THE URBANA FREE LIBRARY
3 1230 00997 4607
W9-AFP-062

MADRID AGAIN

MADRID AGAIN

A NOVEL

SOLEDAD MAURA

Arcade Publishing • New York

Arcade Publishing books may be purchased in bulk at special discounts for sales promotion, corporate gifts, fund-raising, or educational purposes. Special editions can also be created to specifications. For details, contact the Special Sales Department, Arcade Publishing, 307 West 36th Street, 11th Floor, New York, NY 10018 or arcade@skyhorsepublishing.com.

Arcade Publishing® is a registered trademark of Skyhorse Publishing, Inc.®, a Delaware corporation.

Visit our website at www.arcadepub.com.

10 9 8 7 6 5 4 3 2 1

Library of Congress Cataloging-in-Publication Data is available on file.

Printed in the United States of America

Print ISBN: 978-1-951627-12-6
Ebook ISBN: 978-1-951627-27-0

For Marisol

El otro lado está muy cerca de éste, no hay más que alargar un brazo, y ahí está, se toca.
Es ayer otra vez sin haber llegado a ser hoy.

The other side is very close to this one. You can just stretch your arm out and touch it.
It is yesterday again, without ever having become today.

—María Luisa Elío, *Cuaderno de apuntes*

Part I

Part I

1

Metro

. . . memory never stops. It pairs the dead with the living, real with imaginary beings, dreams with history.

—Annie Ernaux, *The Years*

DOWNTOWN MADRID. FOR SOME REASON La Gran Vía comes to mind, even though I never spent much time there. I can see its shadows. I can smell the cologne and the sweat. Mid-1960s. A black-and-white Fellini film, but in Spain, not Italy. The very bright light from the sun. Dark interiors of hallways and churches. Tiny cars. Crowds of people. Women with teased hair washed once a week, sleeveless dresses, kitten heels. Purses clutched tightly. Tanned arms and bracelet-covered wrists. Men in dark suits, narrow ties, and wool hats, despite the sweltering heat. Everyone wearing sunglasses, and gold chains around their necks with a cross or a Catholic medallion. People stopping to light cigarettes. Blind lottery vendors on every corner hawking their tickets with their repetitive cries, "¡*Para hoy*!" The images escape me and go into fast forward as people look worried, laugh, call out to someone, walk quickly, run for the tram, and honk their horns.

This was my family's world. A place where women had crucial roles but few rights. It was the capital city that my mother, Odilia, would leave to move across the world. She was the first person in her family to cross the Atlantic. She went to the United States alone, defying the conventions of a Catholic country ruled by a military dictator and a thoroughly paternalistic culture. Why did she leave? Many good reasons, no matter how you look at it, but it would have been so much easier to stay.

My mother was quite unique compared to her friends, and to her sister. She had always been a big reader, and cherished English and American literature. In the early 1960s she started to meet some of the Anglo expats who were living in Spain. Through them she caught glimpses of other ways to live. I think her first American friend, Edith, had a big influence on her. They met in Madrid in 1965 when Edith worked for the American embassy. My family was predisposed to Anglophilia in all its variants. Though nobody had ever been to the United States, my grandfather was a lawyer for several American companies in Spain. He had studied in England, and his living room was a place in Madrid where guests could drop by for a martini or a bourbon on the rocks.

Edith liked having a local girlfriend from a Spanish family, and my mother spoke English, albeit a Cambridge-inflected, literary version. She was studying English literature, *filología inglesa*, at Madrid's Universidad Complutense. She was one of the few girls from her nun's school, where she had been Head Girl, to continue her studies and attend university. Our family home was close to the American embassy and Edith started showing up every day after work. My grandfather took her on as if she were a third daughter. He enjoyed her sharp blue eyes, dark hair, and sassy repartee. The large flat, with its high ceilings, balconies, and long creaky central corridors, was a welcome respite from Edith's *pensión*, and she was happy to trade in her fixed-price Spanish bar menus, or the stale embassy cafeteria sandwiches, for lunches and dinners carefully planned by my mother and prepared by the family cook who came from a village in Segovia. My mother and her younger sister, Inés, were both in their twenties, unmarried, and living at home. They had studied at the same convent school in Madrid. Their mother died when my mother was four, and Inés barely a year old. My grandfather never remarried. Inés had stumbled through school and dropped out of university, where she had been studying a Catholic version of journalism, a degree called "*El periodismo de la iglesia.*" My mother had been through two serious *novios.* One engagement had lasted four years, but all had come crashing down because of her father's possessiveness and temper.

Edith's and my mother's friendship blossomed as their group of Anglo-Spanish friends grew, and they took trips together throughout Spain and Portugal. Inés, shyer and more conservative, rarely joined them, but eagerly awaited reports and souvenirs when her older sister returned home from these adventures.

The only shadow hovering over Edith's and my mother's friendship was that they were both twenty-eight, a definite cut-off point vis-à-vis the marriageable age. It was the time in life when, as the Spanish expression says, *se te pasa el arroz*—your rice gets overcooked. My mother had truly fancied two of her suitors, but none had lived up to her father's standards, and she felt trapped between her desire for freedom, the pressure to get married, and her father, who once said, "I didn't have two daughters for them to just run off and leave me to grow old on my own."

Thanks to Edith's American outlook (and driver's license), they drove down deserted Castilian country roads in a car borrowed from the embassy, stopping at rural village taverns to eat cheese and bread and drink rough red wine. My mother quickly realized that a certain degree of personal female freedom—which, as a Catholic, Spanish woman raised in the dark years of the postwar, she had never imagined —might in fact be possible. Though local men yelled out the occasional *guapa* and stared plenty when they heard the women speaking a mixture of Spanish and English, they were never really harassed, nor were they ever stopped on the road by the armed *Guardias*

Civiles. These outings were revolutionary. Edith earned money as a part-time chauffeur for the American consulate in Madrid. She was like the plucky Deborah Kerr character in the Michael Powell film *The Life and Death of Colonel Blimp*. My mother had never met anyone like this *americana*. The thrill of being spontaneous, of exploring Spain without the protective gaze of a father, *novio*, priest, nun, general, or husband, was mitigated only by the sense that this lifestyle might come with a price. She couldn't yet fathom how the bill would present itself, or if she would be able to pay when it did.

Between excursions, they went to movies, concerts, and lectures. They started to attend an exiled writer's literature and philosophy talks at the Ateneo and other spaces off campus because that was what cool Madrileños were doing. At least a hundred students crowded the room. The writer was a bit mysterious, which only added to his charismatic allure. Though his name, Zimmerman, didn't sound Spanish, he had been raised in Spain, taught at Oxford, and spent long periods in the United States. Rumor had it that he had been a Republican hero during the Spanish Civil War, and that he had spent years in one of Franco Spain's many prisons before leaving the country, but that was never talked about in the open. Some people said he was a Communist and that he was working against the Franco regime. He spoke English, German, and French. He lectured without notes: on Cervantes, Heidegger, Proust, Neruda, and Borges. The last two were personal friends of his. He couldn't teach at the university or publish because of his political background. He had been officially purged, and his reappearance on the scene had an underground appeal. The male students, many of whom would face prison themselves because of their anti-dictatorship activities, admired him begrudgingly even as they resented how attractive he was to the females. Some of the young men had never left Spain, and some had come from the provinces to study in the capital. One fellow spread the suspicion that Zimmerman was an undercover agent working for the CIA, spying on Spanish youth organizations. How else could one explain his expensive and mysterious comings and goings, his custom-made suits? He even had a car. Nobody really knew anything, but everyone was fascinated by this older, worldly man. My mother and her group were no exception, and often ended up at his *tertulias* having a drink with him and a small group of bold followers at one of the new American cafeterias on the Castellana boulevard.

Change was in the Madrid air. One evening after a post-lecture gathering, Zimmerman offered my mother a ride home. She declined, laughing. "I live two blocks away." He ignored her and opened the passenger side door to his tiny white Seat 600. She got in, smoothed her skirt over her knees, and, embarrassed, looked straight ahead. Suddenly she didn't want to leave that car or go home anymore. But she barely had time to think before he pulled up in front of her house. As she opened the door and started to get out, he said, "I'm leaving to teach in America next year. I know your English is excellent, and that you're working on Emily Dickinson. I'm looking for a teaching assistant to come with me. Many students have applied, but I think you'd be perfect." Standing on the sidewalk, dazed, she turned to look at him, and then shrugged, feigning coolness. "Who knows? By the way, I am not one of the applicants. And I don't know what my father would think about you." She headed toward the entrance of her building, slightly irritated with his tone, and wondered why she had not known about this opportunity to go to America. He laughed, and then she heard him say as he started to drive off, "Well, you'll be hearing from me. I'm not afraid of anyone's father." She was trembling, and smiling, as she walked up the front stairs into her building's lobby.

2

SHE HEARD FROM HIM OVER the summer. She got the position. She was going to America. It all seemed to happen so quickly. The next thing she knew she had official travel documents, a passport, and even her father's blessing. Inés moped around a lot as she watched her sister pack to go so far away, for so long. She dreaded being left without her. "You promise to write to me?" Odilia rubbed Inés's shoulder and planted a kiss on her cheek. "Of course I'll write to you! Don't be silly. I'll only be gone a few months. And don't steal all my clothes and purses . . . Or if you can't resist, be careful with them, or you'll be in trouble." She said this with mock sternness, but the truth was that Inés was notoriously careless, and Odilia imagined her favorite skirts and sweaters, covered with ink stains, or shrunken in the wash. Inés promised, "I'll be careful."

The flight was long, but the excitement made it seem much shorter. The stewardesses were impeccable and it was a wonder that their lipstick, shiny hair, and bright eyes stayed the same over so many hours. Odilia looked at herself in her compact mirror before landing and she thought she looked exhausted. She had been apprehensive about Zimmerman coming to pick her up at the airport, but was then disappointed when he wasn't there. Margarita, a Cuban colleague of Professor Zimmerman, was there instead, and drove her to the Americana Hotel on Sixth Avenue. Odilia was impressed that Margarita drove, and that she knew her way around such a complicated, busy city. They had a sandwich together and walked around Fifth Avenue a bit before Odilia was left alone and given tickets to take the train the next day. She was sad to lose Margarita's company. She stayed up for hours looking out at the skyscrapers. The next morning she took a taxi to Penn Station—trying out her English for the first time, alone—and took a train up the Hudson. It was a long trip. He was at the station the next day waiting for her. He was happy to see her and told her enthusiastically about the sections of his courses that she was going to teach. She was intimidated at the thought of teaching American students. But she had a couple of weeks to prepare, and she would audit his classes so she would know exactly where the students were. As she was swept into becoming a teaching assistant, Odilia did not have much time to absorb the culture shock. She would always remember the first day she stood in front of the classroom to lead a discussion on "El curioso impertinente," one of the interpolated tales from *Don Quixote*. She had stayed up all night preparing her notes and questions, and every time she fell asleep she would wake up again and think of something else the students might ask. She had dozens of notecards on vocabulary alone, not to mention themes and influences. To her shock, the students had also prepared carefully and were generally responsive. She discovered she liked the work, and outside of class the students wanted to know all about life in Spain. She also loved the green lawns and the wooden houses. The simplicity she had imagined when reading Emily Dickinson. The leaves changed colors, the cafeteria had grilled cheese sandwiches, and the drugstore in town had inexpensive things she had never seen, that you could ogle and consider for hours without anyone pressuring you to buy anything. There was also a bookstore where she spent hours sitting on the floor surrounded by American literature. She didn't have much money, but spent what she had on books, and always wrote her name and the date on the first page. She sent dozens of postcards of snow-covered hills and autumn leaves to her family and friends in Madrid.

There were other female teaching assistants who lived on the same hallway, one from Paris and one from Rome. They were also PhD students and stayed up late talking about their classes and plans for the future. They shared a big bathroom with many shower stalls with the students, and each had a basket with her shampoo and soap and plastic flip-flops so their feet wouldn't touch the bathroom floor.

Odilia became somewhat overwhelmed by the newness of everything. What she thought was feverish excitement turned out to be a fever. She went to the infirmary at the university and they gave her the diagnosis. She had come down with mononucleosis. It was not a word she knew. "Round here we call it 'mono' or the 'kissing disease' because of how it spreads," the nurse said jokingly. Her American students teased her and wanted to know who she had been kissing. She feigned offense and told them not to be ridiculous. The kissing disease. It sounded so strange to her, like something fun and frivolous, when she could barely move her legs and her throat was on fire. She was bedridden for weeks. Her friends from her hallway were kind, and Professor Zimmerman discreetly kept his distance, though he called her on the hall phone and sent amusing notes.

She lay in her room for what seemed like endless days and nights. She had never slept so deeply. Some of her students came to visit and brought her food. She kept their gifts of saltines and ginger cookies hidden away on the top shelf of her closet. She noticed that her supplies seemed to vanish mysteriously in the night. As she started to feel better, she awoke one day at dawn and saw a student who lived in the next room quietly rummaging around in her closet. She recognized her, a slim girl with long lank hair and big eyes, but couldn't remember her name. The girl noticed that Odilia was awake and put the crackers back. She turned around and they looked at each other for a split second. Odilia said nothing. There were no more late-night visits. The thieving girl, the fever, the distance from home, and Professor Zimmerman all combined in her imagination. Odilia had a terrible premonition that something deep and irrevocable was being stolen from her in America.

She slowly recovered and went back to teaching. Just as she started to feel like herself again, Professor Zimmerman started showing up at the end of her classes. He always seemed to be waiting for her with a tempting plan to take her for drinks and dinner at the college inn. The Manhattans were strong, and she felt happy sitting with him in front of the fireplace near the bar. The last day of classes, he drove her back to her dorm and told her that he loved her and wanted to spend the rest of his life with her. This was the night before she was set to return to Spain for Christmas. She spent the end of the semester parties with the other TAs and students in a daze.

During her first week back home in Madrid, she was besieged by the confusion Professor Zimmerman had sown in her heart. Sitting in the dining room with her father and sister, she was initially unable to eat the food she had missed so much. But after a time, she readapted and the cocktails and the declarations of love seemed like faint strange memories. She made up her mind to stay home and leave the unsettling American interlude behind. They would have to replace her, but she wasn't going to worry about that. The experience that had started so well had left her shattered: the kissing disease, the unbearable distance from Madrid and her family, and Professor Zimmerman's attention. She would have liked to turn back time, as if it had never happened. In any case, she thought, it wasn't too late. She wrote to him about her decision and said it was final. She tried to keep the tone light but firm, saying her father was not well and that she was needed at home.

But through letters, phone calls, and telegrams, he convinced her to return for the spring semester. He sent a scandalous amount of relentless communications, knowing that each time the postman showed up at her family home, or when the phone rang, she would be terrified her father or sister would find out. Nobody in her house used the phone much; it hung on a wall in a long dark hallway, from where every ring and word spoken could be listened to by all. It was somehow easier to travel halfway around the world again to protect herself and her family from his pestering tantrums. She already had the plane ticket. His last letter was clear: if she didn't return, he would kill himself, but not before sending a letter to her father telling him that he had fallen madly in love with his daughter. She knew she was being blackmailed into appeasement. She told herself that he would never go through with his threats, and that she should stay right where she was in her room in Madrid. But for some reason she started packing, running her hands over the satin compartments of her small suitcase to flatten a few chosen dresses, skirts, and sweaters. Two weeks later she landed at Kennedy airport again, where Professor Zimmerman awaited her triumphantly.

3

DURING THE SPRING, THEY SPENT more and more time together. They visited other Spaniards in the area. He knew everyone. Odilia realized that they were all exiles from the Spanish Civil War, and she was fascinated to discover that they had rebuilt their lives permanently in the United States. She also helped organize an international conference about contemporary Spanish literature in New York. She worked many extra hours, but when she met the writers, it was all worth it. When the event was written up in the *New York Times* she sent the clipping to her father.

It was soon after that Professor Zimmerman insisted they get married right away, in the United States. He explained they could do it in no time at with a justice of the peace. Wouldn't that be wonderful, he said? In America you could get married in the time it took to eat a cheeseburger. People did it all the time. Odilia had always imagined that her wedding would be at a big church in Madrid in the neighborhood where her father lived. She had actually never been too excited about the traditional Spanish society wedding, with the many titled witnesses and all the hoopla. But the idea of this quick wedding made her a bit queasy. He brought the subject up again and again, and said he was starting to make arrangements.

She felt caught, between Professor Zimmerman and her family. How could she get married in the middle of nowhere, like a stray dog?

She asked him to slow down a bit, so that she could at least tell her father and sister. He took her for walks around town and explained that he was trying to turn his current job into a permanent position. Once he did they could buy a house. They had fun walking up and down the town's prettiest residential streets and daydreaming about which house they would buy one day.

Odilia especially liked one with a big porch and a privet hedge that protected the vast lawns. She squinted a bit as she concentrated and tried to imagine living there. Raking the leaves or just sitting on the porch as the mailman or the milkman arrived and said, "Good morning, Mrs. Zimmerman." She imagined all the books they would have, and how they would need to have special floor-to-ceiling shelves made. She asked "Do you think I could still teach a class or two? I guess we wouldn't need the money, but teaching has become a passion for me, and I could write my dissertation at the same time. And we could have children." He replied emphatically, "Of course. That is exactly what we will do. But don't forget, I'll still need your eagle eye and your typing skills for my manuscripts. Children will have to wait. We don't have time now." She wondered what he meant.

One day, as they drove to a local pub for dinner, he announced that his colleague had agreed to be their witness. Professor Buford was a single American man. He taught philosophy. He was young, in the Navy reserves. Once she and Professor Zimmerman had gone to his place for a drink, and when he hung their coats in the hall closet, she saw his neatly pressed uniform in its dry-cleaning bag. He was tall, thin, and wore his hair with a deep side part. He was considered handsome, but Odilia thought his nose was a bit too big for his other features, and the combination gave him a rodent-like air. It was clear that he disapproved of the situation. He worshipped Professor Zimmerman, whom he considered a worldly European mentor, and Odilia sensed that her presence had interrupted an intense friendship. Buford was absolutely immune to her charms, female or otherwise.

Odilia really couldn't be pressed to remember how she ended

up getting married at the home of the justice of the peace. She vaguely remembered his wife. It all happened so quickly, and then they had dinner, without Professor Buford, at the college inn, as usual. They spent the night there. She was still living in the dorm, and Professor Zimmerman was staying in faculty housing for bachelors.

She hadn't told her friends about the wedding, though they must have suspected. The next day she sent a cable to her father and sister in Madrid. She sent another one to Edith. She hated to do so, because she instantly and deeply regretted the wedding. It had been like rushing down the street in the rain and inadvertently stepping into a huge puddle, slipping, and not being able to get back up. When she asked about cabling his family, he said, "They're all dead." That weekend, Professor Zimmerman took her for a two-day honeymoon to Niagara Falls.

Two months later she realized she was pregnant. She hoped the news would bring cheer to her life and her young marriage, but her husband seemed to view it as more of a passing inconvenience than a joy. The funny thing was she found it ridiculous to think of him as her "husband"—he was still Professor Zimmerman in her mind. He made her swear not to tell anybody (as if she would) and promised to find a swift solution. A solution? She saw his declared passion for her waver for the first time. She refused to talk about a solution. She continued to teach all semester. She dragged herself to class—the students were her only consolation. She wasn't really showing yet. What she didn't know was that he was returning to Madrid to teach summer courses. He needed the money and had made all the plans in advance. Why didn't he tell her this before the wedding? Was she going to be stuck in America alone? And then what would happen? She wrote to her father and sister and said she had found a summer research position. They were baffled that she didn't want to come back to Spain and spend July and August in the country with them, which she always enjoyed. And they were looking forward to meeting her husband.

Professor Zimmerman did not want the child, saying he really couldn't afford to start a family just then. He first found her a Catholic home for unwed mothers, where he said she would at least be properly looked after during the pregnancy. During her brief stay there, the nuns changed her name from Odilia to Mary. Mary was a good Catholic name and so easy to pronounce, they said. Sister Catherine said the name would help her assimilate if she was going to stay in the United States. At first Odilia thought the Catholic home was a dreary but safe place for her to wait and have her baby while they figured things out, but she soon realized it was Sister Catherine's intention to give her child to a nice American family that couldn't have their own. After two days with the nuns, she called Professor Zimmerman and said, "Do what you want afterward, but get me out of here now." He found her a room in a small boardinghouse and gave the landlord six months' rent. He came to visit her and promised to find her a good doctor. But he did not change his summer plans. Professor Zimmerman told her, before he left, to call Professor Buford whenever she needed something, but she knew she would never ask him for help. Not even if she was dying.

Edith would be in Spain through the fall, so Odilia was really stranded. She didn't want to tell people about her unhappy situation. Professor Zimmerman sent news from Madrid. Her father and sister also wrote reporting on their unchanging lives. The weather. How everyone missed her. Nothing was altered for them, except the void left by Odilia's absence. It was sad, but sadder yet that they would get used to it. Neither her father nor her sister would raise an alarm or pursue her. Or help her. Or ask questions. How easily she had vanished from their lives. A couple of girlfriends from university sent postcards from their summer travels. She couldn't bring herself to write back to anyone.

And there she was in New York State, far from New York City. She had never imagined that something called "New York" could have nothing to do with the exciting, beautiful parts of Manhattan she knew from so many movies and her two brief visits. Upstate, as they called it, there was no one to tell about her loneliness and fear, or her terrible craving for sweets. At the tiny store a few blocks away from the strange house where she waited for the baby, for the future, and for a chance to go back to Madrid, she discovered tubular striped candy sticks. There was nothing like them in Spain. They were swirly and came in all different flavors and colors. Crazy flavors. Root beer and cinnamon. She lived on these candy sticks while devouring paperback dime novels. It helped her pass the long, lonely hours, waiting for Professor Zimmerman's letters, or the rare phone call which she had to take in the hallway near the stairs. She was well aware that she had regressed to a childlike state. It was as if he had kidnapped her, and she no longer had any agency. The person she had been in Madrid less than a year before seemed like someone else. She had raced around the city, by foot, on the tram, with her high heels, her hair done, and her strawberry-red nail polish. She had lived at home, attended her graduate classes, and gone to parties at embassies and into the countryside with Edith. The future had seemed so exciting, so open. It all seemed impossibly long ago. This was the only real self she had now.

When she was in her seventh month, Professor Zimmerman finally returned from his travels and came to see her. He told her to pack a bag. They went to a house he had rented on a lake somewhere in Connecticut. He drove her in his new dark-green MG convertible. They spent two weeks there. He had been to Scotland, which was inconceivable to her. He had also been to London and Madrid. Now he was with her. What kind of powers did this man have? How had she let him derail her life? He was hatefully well dressed, and brought her two cashmere twinsets, one heather pink, one teal, and a kilt. She wore the dresses she had saved for him. He found her a dentist in Danbury. She had thirteen cavities. It was a shocking number. The dentist cost a fortune.

Sometimes they went out to dinner to the fanciest restaurants he could find, other times he brought food home. In those days, fancy American restaurants had exotic French food that she couldn't eat: frogs legs, escargots. So much melted butter. One night he went out to get pizza and came back with six large pies. For the two of them. Of course they didn't even eat half of one. He always ordered too much, spent too freely, went too far. She wondered where he got the money. In Madrid she had never seen anybody spend so much and couldn't help feeling distaste for his flashiness. She had been raised to value the elegance of austerity. She had never met anyone like him. He was vain. She knew he had chosen a green car to match his eyes. She wished that knowing his weaknesses would give her power, but it didn't. He disturbed her and sometimes she wished, oh how she wished, she had never met him and that she was free and without her enormous belly and everything that meant. But then she would smell his hair, and he would tell her things about Madrid, even about her own family who knew nothing about her pregnancy, and who he had the nerve to keep in touch with. The family he had taken her from. He would gossip about people they knew, and tell her about his publishing projects, and show her his new essays and poems. He made her laugh despite herself. She sat for hours typing up his manuscripts, feeling intellectually stimulated and a part of his world. She was an excellent typist and editor, and more. She often made suggestions that he liked. She knew that she was becoming a better writer in the process, and thought about the poems and articles she would write one day. He said he couldn't live without her.

Professor Zimmerman still swore they would be together forever, but wouldn't it be best to have a child at a more opportune time? Odilia didn't know what he was talking about. Why was their work more important than her life? He explained that he had two major book deadlines approaching, that they were duty-bound to give Spain a better image in the United States and to bring democratic ideals back to their own country. He hadn't just fallen for her; he had chosen her, and she was to be a brilliant magnet for American students. He reminded her of the success of their conference in New York, saying that was just the beginning. She hadn't even known she was being recruited, or that there were any rules to be broken. She thought she had simply come to America to be a teaching assistant. Her family had been pleased for her. Now she was married to him, and he sat there, waving his hands around emphatically, explaining that for reasons entirely related to international politics, it would be selfish of Odilia to have a baby at this time. The new Spain needed young, sympathetic American friends for its future and she was the poster girl. Her students listened to her. As he told her all this, he smoked endless cigarettes and brewed pots of coffee.

He was a lively speaker, and she indulged him, but his political views were not the point. It was true that some of her classmates at the university in Madrid had gone to jail and struggled to change the system in Spain, and she had admired their courage, but to think that she should make a sacrifice in order to keep sowing seeds among a small group of American students was ridiculous. All very convenient for him and the cause. And what about her and her baby?

He had, he confessed, connections with the CIA-run Congress for Cultural Freedom, and it would be bad for his image if people knew he had married and fathered a child with a recruit without even having a full-time job lined up. He would be taken for a fool. She wondered what he really feared most: the CIA or her formidable father. Or nothing at all. She had no time to fear anything.

She was keeping the baby. Once Professor Zimmerman realized she would not budge on that issue, he reluctantly accepted it. But he warned her that she would have to get used to being alone for long periods while he traveled. She assumed he would come back for good in the autumn, but his plans changed. He promised to write to her. And to visit often. Letters. Telegrams. Postcards. Sometimes nothing for over a week. Sometimes ten in one day. For a time she was convinced that these communications were all preludes to his eventual return. They weren't. He gradually vanished. He was the most inconsistent person in the world. She lived through all of this as if she were watching a foreign movie with no subtitles, in which she was the pregnant star.

4

I WAS BORN SOMEWHERE NEAR Canada. It was snowing.

My mother and I. She's told me the story so many times, I feel like I was there. Of course, I was there, but I mean I feel like I remember it, as if I was born aware of the strange situation I had landed in.

During the night when my mother was in labor, the shifts had changed, and a new nurse, at least one my mother hadn't seen before, finally brought me, a screaming infant, into the room. I had been bathed, and a short, thin white ribbon had been tied around the base of my scruffy patch of dark hair, making me look like a tiny blue-eyed samurai. I was a month premature and weighed five pounds, four ounces.

My mother thanked the nurse and did her best to hold me, the first baby she had ever held. The nurse's nametag said DONOHUE. She was large and thick, with ruddy cheeks and short reddish blonde hair. She couldn't help staring at my new young mother, who with her olive skin (as she always describes it), long thin arms, oval face, and almond-shaped green eyes looked, she said, like the image of the Virgin Mary. My mother's black hair was parted down the middle and pulled back with a green velvet ribbon. She said she just wanted to be alone, but the nurse wouldn't leave. Donohue smiled as she shook her head and remarked, "It's such a shame your husband couldn't be here now, Mrs. Zimmerman. Should I call you Mrs. Zimmerman, or just Mary? She's a tiny thing, but what a healthy baby. Anyway, he came while you were asleep. He and a friend . . . another man. They took care of all the paperwork, but they dashed off. He said they were in a big hurry." She had been registered as Mary Zimmerman. At this part in the story, I would always ask: *So my father was there?* This was very important to me. *Yes,* my mother said, *he came. He brought roses. I saved one. I still have it. But,* I asked, *who was the other guy? And why did they leave?* She shook her head. *I'll tell you when you're older.*

My mother smiled faintly at Nurse Donohue and looked out the window at the snow falling in fat, wet flakes. The nurse smiled again, and asked if she had chosen a name for the baby. My mother said "Dolores." She wanted to say *Mi hija,* but she swallowed the words. She had barely spoken to anyone in so long. It was strange to have this Spanish word, her own daughter's name, just pop out of her mouth in front of a complete stranger. It took great determination not to choke on the syllables, and she tried to muster a smile. *Act normal. This is America.* The nurse raised her eyebrows and laughed. "Doh-loh-rays. Well, that'll be a mouthful." It quickly became Lola. Never Lolita, of course, because of the association with the novel.

She wondered when Edith, her only friend in the United States, just back from Spain, would get to the hospital. When her water broke, my mother had hobbled to the phone in the hallway to call Edith's mother's number. She was disappointed that her friend was out, and had to speak bluntly to her mother, who she didn't know: "The baby is coming. Please tell Edith." Her mother said that Edith had driven up to Montreal with some girlfriends to spend the day at the Elizabeth Arden Salon, and that she would tell her as soon as she got back. Edith's mother didn't ask any questions.

But nobody had called back, and the time had come, and it had all happened, so it was just Odilia, me, and the snow outside. My mother marveled at the great distances and the strangeness of Americans. Her friend had driven hours, through the snow, to another country, to have her hair done! Nobody in Madrid could imagine the madness of these people. Edith's hair was in rollers when the beautician brought her a white phone and told her she had a long-distance call from her mother. The minute her hair was set, Edith raced from the salon, got into her new Mustang, and began the long drive south. She was a true Vermonter. The snow was not an obstacle.

As my mother waited, she gestured toward the tall narrow closet and asked the nurse to bring her the small, cream-colored suitcase she had brought. It was a sturdy Samsonite and had been an early gift from my father. He bought it at Loewe in Madrid and the matching cream leather key fob had the store's name written in gold script. It was the perfect suitcase for romantic getaways, discreet and chic. It had reminded my mother of the overnight bag Grace Kelly took to Jimmy Stewart's in *Rear Window*, a movie she had seen with her sister at the Roxy A cinema in Madrid. She had developed such a teenage crush on Jimmy Stewart that she had written him a fan letter, all the way from Spain, and he had responded, sending her an autographed photograph of him and his smiling wife sitting at a table at home drinking coffee. A family man. He had written "For Odilia," and she saved it hidden away in her closet, in a striped hatbox where she stashed her special things. It was still there, in her room in Madrid, with all her clothes, the jewels she had inherited from her long-lost mother, and the life she might not see again.

When Nurse Donohue opened the narrow hospital closet, my mother caught sight of her heavy, ugly rubber snow boots, her dress, her coat, and the silk scarf she had persisted in wearing around her head, although she noticed the American women wore woolen knit hats instead. She had put all her things away carefully before my arrival, and there they still were, immune to everything. She would have to put on those old things again, leave the way she arrived, as if nothing had really happened. Her old Polish American landlord had driven her to the maternity ward in his rusty Buick, chain-smoking during the long, slippery drive. She hoped Edith would get there soon.

The nurse brought her the case, but my mother didn't want to let go of me and asked her to open it. The case popped open, revealing a delicate, soft, white blanket trimmed with pink ribbon woven into the border. My mother reached for the blanket, and the nurse looked puzzled, as underneath there was a second blanket with a blue ribbon, as exquisitely made as the first. My mother spoke slowly in her clearest, firmest English. "Please put the other blanket back in the closet." She fumbled for the right words. "There was a mistake. I thought it would be a boy. Then Dr. Kaufman told me I was having twins. He felt two heads. The other head was a tumor. He removed it. It's been a long night." Nurse Donohue looked concerned as she said, "Imagine that" and put the blanket and suitcase back in the closet, exclaiming cheerfully, "Well, Mary, you can save it for when the next one comes along." She left the room. The snow continued to fall outside, and we were alone. I was wrapped tightly in the blanket she had spent so many hours making.

After what seemed like ages, there was a knock and a "yoohoo" at the door. It was Edith in a plastic rain hat and a heavy coat, carrying a cocktail shaker plus two martini glasses. My mother started to cry when she saw her, then rallied and asked if her hairdo had survived the storm.

The next day, we moved into an attic room at Edith's mother's farmhouse, and *madre e hija* lived discreetly. During that first year of my life, when Professor Zimmerman came to visit those few times, he always brought expensive gifts from Europe: Aquavit, silk scarves, art books, and records—all objects that were incongruous in that Vermont farmhouse. After the visits ended, he would call from far away, and send letters written on hotel stationery. The Algonquin or the Pierre in New York. The Parador de Santiago de Compostela in Spain. Then eventually he disappeared, forever.

5

ON THE DAY I TURNED one, we boarded a plane in New York bound for Madrid. Edith had driven us from Vermont. We had one-way tickets. My mother had packed our few belongings in two suitcases. She was going home and taking me with her. Enough was enough. She needed to build a life and could no longer fathom living at the home of her friend's mother. Edith's mother had taken us in generously and never asked my mother any questions. They had become like family, but we couldn't stay there forever.

Odilia found her home in Madrid unchanged, though Inés had naturally helped herself to her clothes. Neither her father nor Inés asked about my father. Sometimes being from a family that never talked about anything uncomfortable was a blessing. The "American" baby, with her big blue eyes and rosy cheeks, distracted everyone. She may as well have been flown in from Paris by a stork.

But my mother's return was spoiled because she was in pain and losing blood. We had been in Madrid for just a few weeks when she finally made an appointment to see a prestigious doctor, just a few blocks away. She had thought about seeing a doctor in America and had barely been able to afford the airfare to Spain, but now she was glad to be home, where there were people who could look after me in case she needed an operation.

She was dismayed to see that the gynecologist was old, his thinning hair slicked back with brilliantine. He had a dark little moustache and gold-rimmed glasses. There were two pens in the breast pocket of his stiff white lab coat, where his name was embroidered in cursive blue thread.

After examining her and asking a few embarrassing questions about her personal situation, the doctor told her to get dressed and meet him back in his study. Odilia was uncomfortable, but she arranged herself as best as she could before sitting across from the doctor to await his verdict. He asked about her husband, and she hesitated before saying that she was separated, *separada*. This was the most discreet term she could come up with. Divorce was not only a sacrilege, it was illegal in Spain. The doctor looked at her with disapproval. Did he think being separated was also a crime, or did he sense that she was not telling him something worse? She added, as if to explain, that the man in question was American. This did not help. The doctor frowned and raised his hands as if to say, *that's what you get for marrying a foreigner*. In any case, she had been demoted. He was no longer giving her the obsequious treatment he had offered when she arrived, when he thought she was a young society wife from a patrician family.

"I won't have the X-rays for a few days, but I suspect you have several tumors, and I will definitely have to operate. I imagine they are benign, and you are in no danger. In fact, the operation will improve your quality of life dramatically, in every sense. I can schedule you for next week."

Odilia nodded. She asked "Will the surgery affect me in other ways? I only have one child. I just turned thirty-one. Is that it for me?"

The doctor rubbed his hands together and smiled faintly. "Not necessarily. But again, I have to wait to see the X-rays, and then I'll see what's best."

The results came in sooner than anticipated, and three days later she was in the operating room. When she woke from the surgery she was in a dopey, euphoric state from the anesthesia. Inés was sitting next to her wearing a smart houndstooth suit and clutching her purse. The nurse went to fetch the doctor, who strolled in smiling, his hands clutched behind his back in a pseudo casual pose. As he spoke, he rocked slightly back and forth. "So, I am happy to say that you will no longer have any bleeding or pain. The operation was more successful than I had hoped, and I decided to just take everything out to make your life easier. I wasn't sure about the hysterectomy, but for you it was the right choice. It simplifies everything, especially since you've terminated your conjugal life. You'll be on your feet in a week or so, and then you can resume your normal activities. I'm sure you will enjoy having the free time that having only one child allows. You can live your life now. Go to the movies, the hairdresser, go shopping. Plenty of things to keep you busy. You shouldn't have any pains, but I'll expect you to come back for a follow-up visit in a couple of weeks." He smiled, gave a slight bow, and seemed to click his heels together slightly as he turned and left the room. She could hear the soles of his shoes click against the polished, bleached tiles of the hospital corridor.

His words, and the unfathomable news about what he had just done to her body, were unctuously enigmatic, yet everything made perfect sense. Though she had never heard the term *hysterectomy*, she now thought she should have known all along that this was what he would do. Inés, who at twenty-eight had never had a boyfriend, nor been to a gynecologist, understood nothing. She clutched her older sister's hand and smiled widely, her shiny bobbed hair, teased up at the crown, bouncing slightly as she nodded affirmatively. "Well, that's good news! We'll have lots of fun, you'll see. You can just stay at home with little Dolores and live with us. It will be like the old days. I'll come back with you to see the doctor in two weeks."

Odilia, buoyed only by the effects of the drugs in her system, and by the relief that the doctor's face was no longer looming over her, pushed her sister's hand away and clutched the edge of the sheet that covered her distended middle like a tent. "You don't understand anything, Inés. I must return to America, and I am never going to see that doctor again. Please ask the nurse when I can leave."

Inés looked like she was about to burst into tears, and Odilia took her younger sister's hand, "Don't worry," she said, lying, "It's just that I have my teaching job there, and I'm used to my independence now. But we'll stay for a few more weeks, and then one day you can come and visit us in America. You'll like it there. You can wander into all the stores and spend hours looking around and nobody presses you to buy anything. It's like window shopping indoors."

6

MY AUNT INÉS DID VISIT us once or twice in America. I remember being very excited—somebody from Spain coming to see us, trying to connect our disparate worlds. But her trips were short, though I delighted in showing her our local treasures. Maple sugar candy. Covered bridges. It was fun but she didn't seem to want to stay, and I think I wished we could have gone back to Madrid with her.

My mother never learned to drive, which meant we never had a car, and that limited our experiences. Americans don't offer many rides to people, especially to foreigners, so we walked a lot, took a lot of buses and trolleys, and rode subways where they were available. In the Vermont college town of my first years, Middleton, this didn't really matter. We lived close to everything and my mother walked to campus. The one local taxicab drove me to public school every morning. He was an older man, and I thought it perfectly normal to hop into my taxi to go to school, with my little Snoopy lunchbox packed with a thermos of hot chocolate and a peanut butter and jelly sandwich. We went to mass. The church was within walking distance. I walked to Sunday school on my own. I don't remember much about what we discussed or read in those meetings, or how long I attended. I must have been around five years old. There weren't many children in the group. Catholics were a minority in the area. The school was run by a priest, and he made me terrified of Hell. For a couple of years I would ask every grown-up I met if it was all true about Hell, and if we could really burn there. I never once got an answer that put my mind at ease. I insisted on having a first communion in Spain, and my aunt Inés organized one during our next trip to Madrid. I was earnest in my preparations. My cousins came and I had a glimmer of hope that I was en route to becoming a true Spaniard.

Before we really settled in the States, we hovered, and my mother and I spent a few long periods in Spain. I now realize she was trying to figure out just where we could possibly fit in without suffering too much. The truth was, nowhere.

I loved my grandfather's house, where Inés, who never married, lived until she died. My grandfather's chauffeur came to pick us up at Barajas airport, and his two nice sisters—the others were stern and haughty—enjoyed having *una americanita* as a grandniece and bought me beautiful clothes. As soon as I was old enough to wander through the house on my own, I discovered that the kitchen was my favorite part, full of life and the makings of tasty breakfasts—delivered to everyone in bed—and delicious three-course meals. The kitchen was also full of energy, movement, and laughter. It lacked the tension that infused other rooms in the house, though no space was completely free from the ominous threat of my grandfather's moods and impatience. As a toddler, I had loved to crawl down the long wooden hallways, and if I was lucky I would get a splinter. They barely hurt, and led to exciting needles being flamed, and every female in the house paying careful attention to me while Feli, the cook, expertly extracted the tiny wooden shard.

I often went to the market with Feli. Unlike the long New England walks to the fluorescent-lit anonymous supermarket full of iceberg lettuce and ground round, the market in Madrid was just a few sunny blocks away, and it brimmed with competing stalls of meat, fish, vegetables, fruit, olives, and cheeses. Feli confronted the vendors clutching her fat black leather change purse, wearing her black wool coat over a black dress and her black leather soft-soled shoes, which were exactly like the black felt slippers she wore in the kitchen. Her parents had died, and then her husband, and like many Spanish women, she had just found it simpler to stay in mourning clothes all her life. She would argue over every cut of meat and fish, the price and portions on the scale, until everything was exactly right.

Feli wore a copper bracelet that was supposed to fight arthritis that left a green ring around her thick wrist. Her eyes were small, round, deep black, and sparkly. She fascinated me. She had a quick wit and a sharp tongue. She always had the last word, even with my grandfather, who nobody else stood up to. I had no idea that she didn't know how to read, and that she had never been to the beach because she thought swimming in the sea was deadly. We went to the market every weekday, and then I stayed by her side watching the raw materials become the main midday meal. Beef or veal cutlets had to pass through the menacing blows of her large gray stone, shaped like a rather flat Idaho potato. Feli had brought the stone with her, decades before, when my mother was a child, and we only threw it away a few years ago during a once-in-a-lifetime kitchen renovation. Lunch was served in the most beautiful space in the house: a great corner dining room with three balconies. Linen tablecloths were smoothed over *el muletón*, a round piece of white felt that protected the table from scratches or spills. A huge chandelier hung over it.

I was the only child in this household, and I wasn't allowed to go out and play on my own, but with three family members and Feli I was entertained, except for the interminable periods between lunch and cocktail hour, from four to eight in the evening, when the adults all withdrew to their own spaces and the kitchen had been mopped and closed for business until evening. In any case, this life seemed fine to me. I felt at home. My mother only spoke to me in Spanish, so it was my native language. I never understood why we had to leave Spain, as we always did in the end, and go back to America, where we had no family at all, no loving Feli, no playful Aunt Inés, and no spacious home.

We started over in the United States a few times. After we lived with Edith's mother in Manchester, Vermont, my mother and Edith both got teaching jobs at Middleton College, and we moved there and shared a small rental with Edith. Then we rented our own apartment over a garage on a dead-end street. The only positive comparison to this last place was that in the movie *Sabrina*, Audrey Hepburn lived over a garage, but that made sense because her father was a chauffeur. Living over a garage and not having a car was not so charming.

My mother taught novels and poetry, art history, and the Spanish Civil War. I knew that Picasso's *Guernica* had something to do with it, and that an American named Hemingway had been in Spain. She also had LPs of the songs of the International Brigades. I remember the longing, cowboyish sound of one particular song that started "There's a valley in Spain called Jarama . . ." and the flamenco beat of "¡Ay, Carmela!" But I knew nothing about the war, and certainly never thought my family had been affected by it. It was prehistoric for all I knew.

At some point, a medieval history professor went on sabbatical and we moved into his house. Things were looking up. It had two stories, and was full of objects of great interest to me. There was a grand piano, and lots of books about Transylvania and Dracula. I had thought Dracula was just a Halloween costume, but from what I could make out from these books, he was a real person with a history. It was in this house that I watched the *Sound of Music* on a little black-and-white television, and was told the strangest thing: the real Von Trapp family lived in a town in Vermont not far from us, and the two dark wooden chairs with lion paw legs and red velvet cushions on either side of the historian's fireplace had been gifts, many years ago, from the Von Trapps. The chairs had come all the way from Austria.

My mother put a little record player in my room, and I spent hours listening to every word and sound of two records that one of my mother's students had given me: *My Fair Lady* and *West Side Story*. I had also seen the movies on television, and even as a small child I related completely to both stories. I hoped the Waspy medieval history professor would return and rescue my mother, like Professor Higgins did for Eliza Doolittle. *West Side Story* was about Puerto Rican immigrants in New York and the clashes between them and the local Anglos. The female lead looked quite like my mother and was named Maria—as was the star of the *Sound of Music*, come to think of it—and Puerto Rico was like Spain. New York was Vermont. My mother was Natalie Wood.

My story, as far as I could tell, was recast everywhere. I cherished every lyric of my favorite songs, and never tired of them. My mother also loved music, and we each had our own record players and our own tastes. Records were the beginning of some kind of pre-adult identity that filled me with dreams. Edith, who was slightly younger than my mother, gave me some Beatles albums, and from there I eventually moved on to Patti Smith and Blondie, both of whom seemed, each in her own way, to be brave, free, and urban. I knew just through listening that one day I wanted to live in New York and Paris, wear black eyeliner and men's white shirts, and have messy hair.

The professor's house had a kitchen that looked onto a small backyard. In the summer, little hard wild strawberries grew in the patchy grass. I remember a winter afternoon with the snow outside, and my mother baking cranberry bread. This was a novelty. My mother had never learned to cook, or even make a cup of tea, until after I was born. She had quickly mastered bacon and eggs for breakfast, because she thought that was the American way, and that was her repertoire for a few years. The cranberry was an indigenous revelation to her, and cranberry bread was a delicious breakthrough that was very New England-y. We had gone a tiny bit native, and I was comforted by this American activity that was so cozy and delicious.

7

ONE WINTRY DAY I HAD trouble reaching our front door. There was a blizzard, and there were steep stairs and a hilly walk from the spot where I had been dropped off by a friend's mother on our street. I was bundled up, and in one hand, through a thick mitten, I was clutching, like a trophy, a recipe for cookies that we had been given in school. It was mimeographed purplish blue and white. I was so excited and proud to bring this recipe home, and I was terrified that the strong winds would blow it out of my hand, no matter how hard I tried to hold on to it. The paper was already soaking wet.

I saw my mother at the door, and I held the recipe up even higher, so that she might dash down to help me. But before I knew it my hand was empty, and the sheet had blown so far away so quickly that I couldn't see a trace of it. I burst into tears and ran inside, begging my mother to go hunt for this special recipe that I was sure we would never find again. She went out to look, but to no avail.

I was inconsolably sad. Only years later, looking back, did I realize that that morning in my kindergarten class, one of the other children had whispered to me that a classmate was *adopted*. I didn't know what that meant, but she told me it was when your real parents didn't want you, and the state had to find a family to *adopt* you. She also said that it was always a secret, and that if the new parents didn't like the kid, they could return it. Sometimes, she added, the child would go from one *foster* home to another. This information, which fascinated my little classmate, filled me with terror. She was a mean girl, and I knew I shouldn't listen to her, but I couldn't help it. As soon as I heard this, I was convinced that I must be adopted because I didn't have a father. Later in the morning, when we baked the chocolate chip cookies, I had momentarily been distracted from my adoption fears, and had focused entirely on the recipe I would try to triumphantly take home to my mother.

But the recipe was lost to the wind, and from that moment onward, I made my mother promise every day that I wasn't adopted, which she did, faithfully and affectionately.

Yet I still wished my father would appear. My father, or even a father-like figure, I imagined, would bring great happiness to our lives. From television I knew that grown-ups "dated," and this term gave me false hope on one occasion. My mother was going to a dinner with other professors, she said, to meet some "candydates." She said the word in English, with her Spanish accent, and I never doubted that her dinner was to be a combination of very attractive potential suitors and lots of candy. When I asked her eagerly the next day if the "candydates" had been interesting, she shrugged and said they were OK. I was disappointed and eventually figured out my mistake.

It took several years for my mother's English to become more American. I was a simultaneous translator whenever needed. I understood the colloquialisms, the slang, and the thick New England accents that have now almost vanished. My mother proudly told a friend one day that she had "mowed the land" outside our little rental home. Another time she was distraught when a student approached her at the college snack bar. She had successfully ordered cheeseburgers for us and we were enjoying them. The student interrupted and said, "Excuse me, do you mind if I ask where you're from?" That took my appetite away. My mother said "Spain." "Aha," the student said, smiling. She asked, perplexed, how he knew we weren't American. He pointed at our plates: "You're eating your cheeseburgers with a fork and knife."

My mother never spoke about my father, nor did my family in Spain. When I asked questions, I got evasive answers. It was as if he had never existed. At some point I remember my mother talking about adopting a child, an idea I liked, though it also scared me a bit. Of course I didn't know about her surgery and that she could no longer have another baby. But the notion of adoption faded as quickly and mysteriously as it appeared. How could it have ever even been a possibility? By herself she could barely raise me and teach at the same time. When I was three or four my mother asked one of her colleagues, who had children my age, for advice about writing a will. If she didn't have a will with a designated guardian for me, he said, and anything happened to her, I would become a *ward of the state*. He also seemed to be offering himself and his wife as legal guardians, just in case. They had two girls who were a bit younger than me. Somehow I overheard this conversation, and though I was very little, I immediately understood everything. Ward of the state—of Vermont—words I had never heard before, were perfectly and terrifyingly clear to me. To have these people as my legal guardians was something I was not prepared to accept, however hypothetical or well-intentioned it was. Nor was my mother, and when she made the will, she appointed Edith and my aunt Inés in Madrid as my guardians. Just in case.

This terrifying eventuality of my mother's possible death and its consequences descended into our tiny living room like the looming tornado from *The Wizard of Oz*. The lawyer who drafted the will was a kind, tall, rangy man with tanned skin and white hair. He was a part-time lawyer and full-time beekeeper who made house calls, and with every professional exchange came a new large jar of Adirondack honey. The honey, the colleague, and the will were all part of a dark scenario that hinged on a circumstance that, to me, was unimaginable: my mother dying and leaving me alone.

This took place in the house my mother rented from the medieval history professor whose family had come over on the *Mayflower*. It was the most profound fear I had felt, but there had been others. One sunny day we looked through the window and saw a big car pull up to the curb on the street where we lived. Two men wearing suits, hats, and trench coats got out of the car, one of them smoking a cigar, and to our disbelief they slowly made their way to our front door. The doorbell rang. My mother told me to go upstairs while she spoke to them. It took longer than I hoped. If I overheard anything, I don't remember. When I asked her what it was all about, she simply said, "It was the FBI. But they were looking for someone else." I probably didn't know what FBI stood for, but in the context the acronym was somehow self-explanatory..

I had a blue passport with an eagle on it, but my mother had a green card. My mother and I had to go through different passport lines when we entered and left the United States. Customs officials, both in Spain and in the States, lorded over areas of high anxiety where my mother always risked getting a migraine. She traveled with a special medication and a crafty little plastic cup that collapsed like an accordion into a flat object when not in use. I disliked this cup and the medicine because they were associated with feelings of precariousness, the sense that we had always just made it past the police by the skin of our teeth. The trips were all perfectly legal, yet in my memory they were very tense and unpleasant. Even when we had arrived and were out of the airport, there was no real relief because every single trip we took, whether to or from Spain, was always part of an eventual round trip. We never stayed anywhere permanently.

When I was older, my mother told me that that the first time we left Spain, when I was still a baby, the Spanish police refused to let her take me out of the country because she didn't have the right paperwork. Another time—and this I remember vaguely because I must have been eight or nine—we were stopped when we arrived in Spain because there was a search warrant out for a mother-daughter pair whose description we apparently matched. I lolled about and felt scared and clumsy while we were detained and searched and my mother was interrogated. It was the first time I knew our fate was not up to her, and that anything might happen. We were let go, of course. And it wasn't until many years later that my mother told me about her immigration interview in New York when she was pregnant and had decided to stay in the United States. She wore a nice dress, a raincoat, and her pearl earrings. They asked her what she planned on doing with herself, and how she was going to make money. She said she didn't know. The pudgy, white-haired, blue-eyed agent looked her up and down through his smudged glasses: "Well, are you going to walk the streets?" My mother was stumped, though she understood the literal meaning of all the words. The insinuated colloquial meaning crept in more slowly, but with violent clarity. She felt her hands start to tremble, looked defiantly at the officer, and said, "I don't understand the question."

For so long I thought that these horror stories were a part of a world that was safely gone, but I was wrong.

8

I HAD AIRSICKNESS FOR YEARS. With all the trips back and forth, I spent many hours of my early life perched over Iberia, TWA, or Pan Am motion sickness bags, swallowing and trying not to throw up. Someone told me that throwing up on a plane was worse than not throwing up, because throwing up would just bring on new waves of nausea. I don't remember anyone else being sick on these flights and it was humiliating. The mere thought of the airplane, the sight or taste of those medicinal chewy orange children's Dramamine pills, or the overpowering smell of American brewed coffee, in glass pitchers that the stewardesses carried up and down the aisles repeatedly, that wafted out of the airborne kitchenette: any of these could set me off. Turbulence was also a sure trigger, bringing on motion sickness combined with the firm conviction that we were going to die.

But I recovered quickly after each flight. As soon as we arrived at my grandfather's house in Madrid, always in the early morning, no matter how sick I had been on the plane, I would tear down the long, dark hallway to the bright kitchen to see Feli and ask for a chorizo sandwich. My aunt Inés always asked eagerly if we had jet lag, a term she learned from a magazine and found cosmopolitan. In response, to her disappointment, we always shook our heads. My mother was tired after the trip, but I was raring to go. We had no idea what jet lag was.

Francisco Franco's minister of tourism had coined the catchy slogan "Spain is Different," and during the years we spent there, I would have agreed. The bathroom at my grandfather's house fascinated me. The toilet was in a separate room, and to flush one had to pull a chain. The loo paper was rough and gray, or sometimes bright pastel pink or blue. It was never white. Cotton balls were also dyed in pastel colors. Many families bought cologne in liter-size bottles. It was a household staple, like laundry detergent. My grandfather was tall, and he wore a suit and hat for his morning stroll through the neighborhood. He carried a cane and had a putty-colored patch covering one of the lenses of his glasses. He had lost an eye in a botched cataract operation. He had involuntarily moved or twitched, against the doctor's strict instructions that he keep the eye completely still. This may have been typical of early cataract surgery, but in my mind, there was something very sad about this story. My elegant, vain grandfather—whose gaze peered commandingly out of the photographs from his youth – was very elderly by the time I was born.

Lavender and citrusy colognes were popular, but unfortunately many people wore uniforms that were never changed or cleaned frequently enough. It was a key part of the dictatorship culture. A literalization of uniformity. A militarization of civilian life. People who worked in shops wore uniforms, and so did taxi drivers. Even my aunt, who worked as a guide in the Royal Palace, had a summer and winter uniform. I loved her job, and she used to take me to work with her all the time. I could run around the Palace to my heart's content, and the guards would just wink at me and give a piece of candy. My favorite thing was ducking under the thick red velvet ropes and looking up at the Tiepolo frescos on the ceilings. I also liked the parts of the tour when Inés explained that most of the paintings on view were reproductions, and that the originals were at the Prado. I assumed that the tourists would never know this and that Inés had real inside information. She led groups of twenty to a hundred people at least twice a day. She never knew how many would show up, and she was prepared to guide the groups in English, French, or Spanish. She sometimes made friends with the visitors, and through her we met a very kind Argentine couple who lived in Boston. When Inés came home for lunch in her official garb, which included a pillbox hat and white gloves, she was served by a maid in a uniform with a white apron. And people smoked liked fiends. My aunt was a chain smoker and most of the guests who came over for drinks also smoked. There were wonderful heavy enameled cigarette lighters. My favorite one was in the shape of an elephant. There were silver cigarette cases and ashtrays everywhere, constantly emptied and cleaned. It seemed like more of an art than a vice. I thought Inés was so cool. She stayed under my grandfather's roof and eschewed the responsibilities of being a grown-up. This kept her somehow extra youthful. She was absent minded and once or twice came home from walking one of the dogs without the dog, though it all worked out in the end. She smoked, curled up on the couch, surrounded by books on Flemish tapestries, the Spanish royal families, painting, and decorative objects. She was sometimes overwhelmed by the scope of what she thought she should know. She dreaded the question some conniving or innocent tourist might pose and show her up in front of the crowd.

I've wondered what it was like for my mother to be under my grandfather's roof again. And what it was like to share an adult life with her sister, who never married. Seen from my limited American perspective, life in that house seemed so regimented, and I had no idea how anybody felt about anything or anyone.

In New England everybody wore comfortable tumble-dried clothes, and people were in and out of each other's houses at all hours. Martinis, whisky sours, cigarettes, station wagons, and barbecues ruled the day. There was no such thing as "organic" meat, just hotdogs and burger patties, ketchup and relish. The food at other people's houses tasted faintly of dishwasher detergent to me. It was off-putting and unfamiliar. Children—and adults—had Cheerios for breakfast and lunch, and walked around barefoot in the summer. In the winter people threw a coat on over their pajamas to drive to a convenience store to get coffee and the newspaper. Though it was a college town, it was rural. It was America.

At our home in Madrid, nothing was spontaneous. There was a living room where the grown-ups had drinks, and a breezy sitting room for the women, where the television was. There was only one Franco-run state channel. My grandfather had his large study. We only gathered for meals. Everybody was dressed and groomed at all times, unless they were in the privacy of their own rooms. Nobody from the family ever went into the kitchen except for me.

My mother didn't work when we lived in Spain, and I was either not yet in school or on vacation. In the mornings, after my adventures at the market with Feli, my grandfather, who was long retired by then, and my mother would walk down the Calle Serrano or Claudio Coello with me to the Retiro Park. Once there, we would visit the rose garden, and then we would stop at one of the many bars with the plastic chairs and tables on sandy plots between the park's lawns, paths, and avenues. I would have a Coke and a bag of potato chips, most of which were broken into crumbs to feed the sparrows that hung about. Then we would walk back for lunch that was always served at 2:00 p.m. sharp.

I loved the evenings in Madrid when my mother went out with her old friends or cousins. It gave me a glimpse of the person she'd been before America, before me, the person I hoped she might become again. She was always very pretty, beautifully and simply dressed, slender and long legged, with dark shiny hair and delicate features. In Middleton she had made good friends, some who had children my age, but in America she was often harried by her classes, bundled up for the snow, or concerned about money. She sometimes wore an expression of worry, a kind of frown, that as a child I often begged her to replace with a friendly American smile. Things had been hard for her since she left Spain, and I unconsciously suspected that my existence was to blame. In Madrid, when people came over for lunch or drinks, and especially when she went out to dinner, she was a different person. Not only was she vivacious, smiling and laughing, but she seemed downright glamorous, carefree, and slightly haughty. It was like having two mothers, and though the other mother had been through so much—and I couldn't live without her—I selfishly preferred the evening-going-out-in-Madrid version.

If my mother was happy, I was somehow absolved. Like a gambler, I placed many emotional bets on her late-night outings in Madrid, hoping they would stick so that we would never have to get on another airplane. But we always went back. I was too young to fathom that a return home might also have a dark side for her, that it could be oppressive. She could never explain to anyone what really happened between my father and her. But I sensed she belonged in Spain and that I had somehow taken her away from her real home. I couldn't yet imagine that, in a way, she had needed to leave Madrid.

9

The Long Shadow
This was a poet
EMILY DICKINSON Richard Chase
THE POEM ITSELF
HAIKU
INTERPRETATIONS OF AMERICAN LITERATURE
The Editing of Emily Dickinson
The Puritan Oligarchy

AFTER I WAS BORN, MY mother abandoned her plan to pursue her doctorate in American literature with a dissertation on Emily Dickinson. It took her several years to fully dismiss the idea. At home she seemed to have every book ever published of Dickinson's work, and she bought all the critical studies and biographies that came out. On a trip to Madrid she went back to the university to speak to a professor at the English literature department where she had done her coursework. She had rewritten the beginning of her thesis to show to him. It was a big step for her to try to piece her life back together. The professor she met with, an old man, told her not to bother him again until she had a finished product of at least 500 pages to show him. But even then, he said he wasn't sure they would be able to readmit her after such a long hiatus. I remember her sadness after this meeting.

Without a PhD, she could only teach part time at Middleton. When I was seven we moved to a town near Boston where she was offered a permanent teaching job at a private school. I never asked why we moved, and I didn't want to go. I don't think she wanted to leave either. It made me feel untethered. Middleton and Madrid were just about as much variety as I could take. On the big day, when the moving truck arrived at 6:00 a.m., I was covered in red spots and had a high fever. Chicken pox. It was my unconscious protest. We moved anyway.

Not having a car in the new town was difficult. There was nothing but churches and a convenience store and it required a twenty-minute walk to reach them. Even the post office was in another town. Sometimes as we trudged along people we knew would drive by, honk, and wave. They were often going to the same supermarket, and we would see them driving off again, the car loaded up with brown bags, as we arrived. In New England people believed fiercely in Emersonian self-reliance, and surely thought we were getting some much-needed exercise. My mother, resigned to the fact that nobody would ever help us, or even give us a lift, would wave back with her best American smile. I never understood how people could just drive by and wave as we, carrying our bags, slipped and slid down the snowy sidewalks, which were never cleared because we were—as far as I could tell—the only pedestrians in town.

For the first time I felt like we were foreign, and that having a single mother with a foreign accent was shameful. I tried to change my name from Lola to Rose, but it never stuck. There were two days that were unbearable for me: Parents' Day at school, and the national holiday, Father's Day. Everybody else had a father, or so it seemed to me. I lied and told some classmates that my father was dead. It was the best story I could think of, and it seemed it might gain me sympathy. It couldn't even really be called a lie, because I didn't know the truth. And indeed I secretly hoped he was dead, because that was the only excuse that would justify the fact that he was not with us, driving us to the supermarket in a Volvo station wagon, carving Thanksgiving turkeys, and putting up the Christmas trees. These were the images of families I had from the L.L. Bean catalogue that fascinated me. But even more secretly I suspected he wasn't dead, and this led me to continue to wait for him, even though I knew, within the deepest level of knowing I could access, that if he hadn't come back by then he never would.

Though the new town was quite pretty, it was a school town,

and many of the grown-ups seemed sad. Many of the teachers were spinsters and bachelors; some had families. Cottage cheese and black coffee was a common grown-up lunch. There was a stern ambiance at the school, which I sensed with alarm even as a seven-year-old. Everyone, including us, wore scratchy Shetland sweaters. The Fair Isle knit was the big look for girls. People were not as welcoming as in Vermont. There were exceptions, of course, and a few people invited us to dinners and holidays and were lively and wonderful hosts. There was an elderly female French teacher whom I adored. The school had originally been all boys, and the blueprint endured. The smell of the gym, the bad food, the lack of restaurants, cafés, or stores of any kind in the town. Some of the administrators had faint British accents that seemed to endow them with extra power. My mother was a young, extremely gifted teacher beloved by her students. Yet the transition was not easy. There were new customs, and she was assigned Dickensian chores. For example, though she did not have a car, or drive, and had to look after me by herself, she was at school daily from 7:45 to 3:15, at which point she walked a mile back home, but at 5:00 p.m. (which was dark for much of the school year), she had to return alone every day to the main school building to make sure all the windows were locked for the night.

I walked to school and back with my mother, and then on my own when I was older. I walked to my piano teacher's house in the afternoons. I loved to play the piano. Anything musical was always a great joy to me. My teacher and my mother said I had a gift for music, and this made me feel very special as I prepared for recitals. On Saturdays we took public transportation to a nearby town that had a mall. It was six miles away and the trip took less than fifteen minutes if you went by car; by bus it took us nearly an hour and a half each way. The bus stopped all the time. I knew that if it didn't, it wouldn't be accessible to us, but that was no consolation. We had to walk fifteen minutes to the bus stop, and never knew exactly when it would come, or if it would show up at all. Apparently there were different schedules for weekdays, holidays, and seasons, and the information wasn't posted anywhere. Also, you needed exact change, which was a complicated combination of nickels, dimes, and quarters multiplied by two, one set for each of us. If a dime went missing we couldn't get on the bus. My mother's education in regimented Spain had made her fearful of uniformed officials, including the bus drivers of our suburban American route. After each of these day-long outings, we were exhausted.

On certain days, without explanation, the same route required that we change buses in a town called Quincy, at the Quincy Center Station. This would add another half an hour each way. The station was full of sad Vietnam vets in wheelchairs (often missing limbs), bag ladies, and stranded people, along with revved-up teens with feathered hair, nylon jackets, and huge combs in their back pockets, smoking and snapping gum at the same time. There were many small bottles of cheap booze in brown paper bags in people's pockets, plastic purses, or worn out Filene's Basement shopping bags.

Sometimes we only went to Quincy, which was forty-five minutes away on the bus. The attraction there was a department store outlet called the Bargain Basement. It had no windows and little ventilation. The only place to eat after shopping there was a dark wood pub-like coffee shop, part of a chain, called the Pewter Mug. It served navy bean soup and Reuben sandwiches that had left their Jewish ghetto to become part of the American mainstream. I remember the silent footsteps of the waitresses in their burgundy polyester uniforms with nametags, pantyhose, and white lace-up shoes on the navy patterned wall-to-wall rug. There was a shamrock motif, and paper doilies on the tables near the worn little metal milk pitchers and plastic artificial sweetener and sugar holders. We learned about Quincy from my mother's Cuban colleague whose own mother lived in a small apartment there. We went to see her once. Born in Havana, she had moved to be near her only son, and she lived alone. He had been brought to the United States during Operation Peter Pan in the early sixties. I didn't know what any of this meant then, but it was hard for me to imagine that anybody could be better off in Quincy than in a place called Cuba.

The Bargain Basement was not like more modern outlets that simply have surplus merchandise. This store was frequented not only by a couple of displaced Spanish speakers like us, but also by car-owning thrifty locals. It was full of rejected merchandise. The key word on the labels was IRREGULAR, abbreviated as IRR. People would spend their day off sorting through trousers to make sure the legs were the same length, or microscopically examining the snag on a sweater to see how easily it could be repaired. There were clothes for the whole family. Some items were extremely irregular and had a further discount. Those prizes were only for the most talented menders and launderers.

Quincy made me want to go back to Spain, where there was no wall-to-wall carpeting, and where the people we knew weren't hell-bent on buying and accumulating inexpensive ugly things. The only item I remember from this store was a pair of gauchos. Gauchos were all the rage, a kind of skirt split to look like a trouser. All the girls slightly older than me had them, as did a few of the more fashion-forward in my class. I finally convinced my mother that I urgently needed gauchos, and we made our way to Quincy one day to find them. I don't recall what, if any, irregularity they had. They may have been forced to exit the normal retail world because of their color: brick red. So after much complaining, and a round-trip bus ride, I had a pair of gauchos I couldn't wear. They didn't go with anything. And it was unimaginable to spend another Saturday returning them.

Every time the bus left Quincy proper, it took a turn near the John Quincy Adams House. I didn't know if he was born there, lived there, or both. But it was a pretty house, white, and set off from the town that shared the president's name. Many people on the bus carried large clear bags full of empty cans. They went around collecting them and took them to some supermarket to reclaim five-cent deposits.

Compared to Quincy, another mall in the unfortunately named town of Braintree—also accessible by bus—was like Harrods. It was covered and warm and had cosmetic counters, which fascinated me. Heavily made-up smiling ladies in floral shirts and pantsuits offered to spray you with Estée Lauder perfumes. And there was a shop that was the closest thing around to a gourmet store called Hickory Farms, where we bought what to us were exotic snacks like banana chips and port wine cheese. We had lunch there at a restaurant called the Magic Pan, which had the most European offerings around for miles: crepes, potage St. Germain (split pea soup with sherry and sour cream), and a green salad with slivered almonds, tinned mandarin slices, and vinaigrette. There was also a store called the Lodge that had coveted rugby shirts, corduroys, and jeans.

When we made it into Boston there were many hits and misses in our car-less explorations. We took the T, which also involved a long walk, and got off at Newbury Street, where my mother had discovered a good hairdresser, and where I had found vintage and preppy clothing stores. But our special place came to be Cambridge. We got there by trolley, and then the Red Line train. There were many homeless people around Harvard Square, which made me sad, but also it had bookstores, a Spanish restaurant called Iruña, and a gourmet store with European products called Cardullo's. Though I never pressed for more information, I had heard my mother say once that my father had loved Cardullo's, and that the three of us had been in Cambridge together for a few days when I was a baby.

Iruña, a small place with wooden tables and chairs, was the only Spanish restaurant we knew of. Americans didn't eat Spanish food then, and the only dish my mother made at home was *sopa de ajo.* The simple and delicious garlic soup had few ingredients: garlic, bread, Spanish paprika, water, salt, and olive oil. During one of our trips to Spain my mother bought little wooden spoons and we ate the soup with these out of brown earthenware bowls she also brought back. In my family's house in Madrid we used silver, and antique French china. In America we had become folkloric Spaniards, nostalgic for a fantasy of an unadulterated culture. At the Iruña restaurant I remember having *champiñones al ajillo*, mushrooms in garlic sauce, that were delicious and tasted of our dislocation. I was always shy about speaking Spanish at the restaurant, as if it would be a test of my authenticity.

We never would have admitted that we acted like exiles. Exiles for us were older and somehow different. When my father first lured my mother to America he took her to visit a Spanish professor and his wife in Western Massachusetts. They had never gone back to Spain after the Civil War. Thirty years had passed. They relished my mother's visit. Not many young Spanish women from prominent families had graced their table. My mother was shocked at the *Spanishness* of their house. Their clothes seemed to have remained intact from the 1930s, and all the surfaces of the living room were covered by ivory-hued crocheted doilies the wife had made. Photographs of their ancestors in silver frames abounded. The wife had made *rosquillas de santa clara*, traditional anise-flavored biscuits shaped like donuts, covered with a lemon glaze, and served them with *chocolate*—the thick, Spanish hot chocolate. They played *pasodobles* on the record player. My mother said the house was a tract house—she described it as a shoebox—built alongside many identical structures, but that inside it was like a modest old Spanish prewar home. She felt that they had clung desperately to their identities, and that they also wanted to show her—freshly arrived from the homeland—that they hadn't lost their ways. My mother was very moved by them. She remembered the husband saying that all he wanted was to be buried in Spain. Those were exiles. We were something else. I wasn't sure just what.

As we walked to and from the bus, school, or anywhere else around the Boston area, my mother would tell me about her childhood in Spain. The stories had no particular start or finish—she could get into them at any point, waiting for the bus, or during a long walk to the market on an uneven sidewalk crunchy with fallen leaves. She loved the Madrid apartment she grew up in. Though the flat had plenty of space, she and

Inés shared a bedroom for many years. They used to whisper into the night. When they ran out of conversation, Inés would say "Odi?" and my mother would say "*¿Qué?*" and Inés would respond, "*Nada.*" Inés was afraid of the dark and sometimes they held hands from bed to bed until she fell asleep. My grandfather, who went on hunting and fishing trips every weekend, was rarely home and as the elder sister, Odilia was the queen bee. When she wasn't in school she was fascinated by the running of the household. Once a year she joined in the waxing of the wooden floors, shimmying on rags down the central hallway and into the smallest corner of every room. She also liked polishing the silver, and picking the stones, insects, and twigs out of the dried lentils before they could be soaked and set to simmer with chorizo, onions, and garlic. There was a *cuarto de los armarios*, a dark, high-ceilinged walk-in closet that fascinated her, and later terrified me. This room held all the sheets, blankets, and towels, but went far beyond the scope of what we consider a linen closet. It was also the home of the *colgaduras*, which were massive heavy hangings in royal blue with gold trim that took up more square feet than the average New York City one-bedroom apartment.

These *colgaduras* had originally been made for my great-grandparents' balconies to celebrate royal occasions. They were first used in 1906 in honor of the wedding of King Alfonso XIII to Princess Victoria Eugenia of Battenburg. The wedding was held at the Basilica of San Jerónimo in Madrid, very close to my great-grandparents' home, which still stands on the corner of Alarcón and Antonio Maura. Everyone who lived in the neighborhood dressed up their buildings to celebrate the royal marriage.

My grandfather, the eldest of eleven children, inherited the hangings, yet their purpose would change. As of 1931, Spain no longer had a monarchy. After the Republic and the Spanish Civil War, the royal family were in exile. Franco's dictatorship celebrated its victory every year on April 1. On the eve of this date the family would bring out the vast *colgaduras* and carefully hang them, one for each of the thirteen balconies. My grandfather was not a supporter of Franco, but peer pressure was a force to contend with during the war and the regime. My mother relished this household tradition, independent of its political meaning. When my grandfather was old and fragile, their building was sold to a developer, and he and my aunt moved to a smaller apartment near the Retiro Park. My mother and I were in the United States at the time. My aunt Inés was unable to cope with the downsizing and hated the experience of leaving her lifelong home. Her vengeance was wrought by leaving behind almost everything that could have mattered most in personal or economic terms: French antiques, thousands of valuable books, letters between my grandparents, and the *colgaduras*. Much later in my life, I met a well-known architect who had been hired to gut the building and turn it into smaller flats. He told me that in his first walk-through he had seen books with my grandfather's *ex-libris* scattered on the floor, antiques, and more personal effects in my family's storage space in the attic. He had taken one book for himself as a souvenir, but he was just hours ahead of the wrecking ball, and nobody even stopped to loot the remains. Everything was destroyed.

My grandfather lived another few years after the move. My aunt looked after him, with help, when he became very ill. They started to pray the rosary in the late afternoons. My aunt's bed was eventually covered with rosaries hanging off all four antique bedposts.

We would never have used the *colgaduras* again—Madrileños now only kit out their terraces, balconies, and windows with flags of different kinds during major soccer events—yet somehow I wish I still had even a thread of one of them. I do have a rosary that my father gave my mother. It is made of rosewood and has a little leather pouch. Today, decades later, it still has a wonderful aroma.

None of my classmates in the Boston suburbs were hearing stories about *colgaduras*, nor were they making pilgrimages to eat mushrooms at Spanish restaurants or buy foreign books on Saturdays. They weren't longing to go back to another country. I felt the need to connect with my history. My friends were playing tennis, ice-skating, skiing, or at their beach houses. I always secretly hoped that, in the long run, I wouldn't have to fit into their world. I sensed that if I tried too hard, I would damage part of myself.

I still missed Vermont, where we had somehow blended in, where I had been younger and more innocent. In the private school world near Boston, I felt crushed by the intransigent forces of conformity. I no longer hoped my father would return one day and complete our family romance. Then my mother took me aside one evening and told me that she had found out that he had died, in Cuba she thought, and that she didn't want me to tell anybody. My only association with Cuba was my mother's colleague, and something I'd heard of called the Bay of Pigs. And Communism. Having recently, along with my entire school, watched the television film about nuclear war, *The Day After*, my Cold War fears exploded. "Was he a Communist?

Is that why the FBI once came to our house?" I asked, nearly hyperventilating from this fearsome possibility. "No, not really," my mother said. Not really? What was she talking about? "He wasn't really a political person," she said. "I mean, he got swept up in things, but he was fundamentally a poet and an intellectual. And of course he'd been an anti-Fascist during the war. His family was Jewish." What war? I thought she meant Vietnam. That was the only war I knew about. I didn't know if this information made things better or worse. I didn't understand how he could have traveled to Cuba. I knew it was not allowed. She shrugged and said, "Maybe from Mexico. I don't know." His death led to many difficult conversations and tears. I was sure that we were now definitely going to burn in hell, and how was I supposed to get over that? I was inconsolable.

I was still young enough to believe that I had missed some kind of happiness and security by not knowing him, even though the more I heard, the less he was like the father I had dreamed about. Good American that I was, I wanted to go and speak to the school counselor, who was a nice lady married to the squash coach. My mother shook her head. I told her I would go live with my grandfather and aunt in Madrid, that at least they weren't Communists. "That," she sighed, "you can be sure about." At least in Madrid I might have a shot at a life that would take me to heaven.

All of this was to be our secret, she said, and I might not understand its significance for many years. She gave me things she had been saving for me, photos of my father, of the two of them together, and thick packets of airmail correspondence between them. She gave me the little plastic bracelet the hospital had put on my wrist the day I was born. She told me it had snowed, and that the doctor who had delivered me said I looked like a little Spanish princess from a painting. She gave me the baby blanket she had knitted for me, and ten birthday cards, in their envelopes, that my father had sent me over the years, all postmarked differently with no return address. In each he had put a $100 bill, and had sent *muchos besos* to *la piqui*—his nickname for me, which my mother also used—and *su madre.* She had kept everything in a small white Samsonite suitcase with its own little key. I had never seen these cards, and had always wondered at the $100 my mother gave me on my birthdays. She told me I didn't have to look at any of it now, but that it was all mine, forever, and I could do what I wanted with it.

Late that night, alone in my room, I opened the suitcase. Everything was so beautifully organized. I randomly opened bits of the correspondence. A short note from my mother, written to my father after she returned to Madrid, during her initial time with him in the United States. She was clearly trying to avoid him.

> *I told my father about the possibility of returning to complete my year in America. He is not enthusiastic. He and Inés are so glad to have me back home, that I can't imagine leaving them again, no matter how much I miss you, and don't think that I don't. Don't be angry. My father is 75 years old. It weighs on me, and I can't fight it.*

If only their relationship had stopped there. If only she had broken up with him then, he wouldn't have ruined her life. But then I wouldn't exist.

Soon after that letter, my mother returned to America to

rejoin Professor Zimmerman. It went against all she believed in; against the way she had been brought up. How much did she know about my father and what he did in America? Who was this man who would permanently uproot her life, marry her, and vanish?

Then I found two other letters written by my mother that were undated. In these the tables had turned. They were married, he was away. She was already pregnant with me and alone, stuck in upstate New York. My father was back in Madrid working. I was moved by her isolation and loneliness and the love and devotion in her tone.

> *Everything is fine. A quiet life. The weather is good and there's light in the "living room," as they call it here. The street is pleasant, and I take walks around the block, not too far because I get tired. I knit, I sew, I've put my books out, and I'll let you know if I actually get any work done, but I get tired if I sit too long. I have lunch at noon. Sometimes I put the television on, and yesterday I watched quite a bit to hear the news about Robert Kennedy. It's so horrible, there are no words to describe it. The truth is that death and life are so close together, and it's much easier to live without thinking about it.*
>
> *I'm back now. I left you for a bit because the neighbor took me to the "basement" to show me how the washer works. I hope I'll be able to figure it out. Tomorrow I'll go down and tackle domestic life, which I now realize I didn't do while you were here. I've hardly taken care of you, I've been a terrible housewife and I'm sorry, but I'll do better next time. I wish (that's putting it lightly) that you were*

here. I think of you a lot. I don't think much about myself, and I think of the baby all the time.

I think I have reached a certain serenity, sometimes it is tinged with sadness, sometimes with joy, but it is serenity all the same—achieved little by little, with great difficulty.

The last one was the most painful to read:

Thank you for the three letters. I think you guessed that I was depressed and that's why you wrote me so much. Yesterday my little walk was longer than usual. I went to the shops and looked at things. I bought blue wool to make the baby a blanket, since Dr. Spock's book says that the best ones are "knitted ones." I didn't feel like cooking, so on the way home I stopped at a cafeteria and had my classic cheeseburger—which was really good—and an immense strawberry milkshake. These are the only things I know how to order. I came home and read your letters, and then I read them again. I lay down for a bit and then started the little blanket. I had dinner, and took a bath and washed my hair, which felt great. And there you have my day. I just crossed it off the calendar, a schoolgirl habit that always consoles me. Four weeks have gone by, but the problem is that the remaining ones will seem longer because of my impatience.

I don't really need any shoes or clothes. My good dresses, the "maternity" ones, are pretty much untouched. I'm saving them for when you're here, and because the weather's been so bad I almost always go out wearing my trusty raincoat which I consider the invention of the century.

I'm sorry to hear you can't sleep. Madrid must be unbearably hot at night. I know you're working fiendishly. The baby and I aren't any help at all, but we send you what we have, love and kisses.

I couldn't read any more of these. My mother alone, reading Dr. Spock. Waiting for letters from my father. Eating a cheeseburger by herself. Saving her nice dresses for his return. There were many more letters like these. He saved them all. She asked him to return them to her. The very least he could do. She had hers and his. Letters, photos, and me.

By the next year, I had read Anne Frank in school and thought that having a Jewish father was fascinating. I no longer thought about hell. I had favorite teachers and loved English, French, history, and drama. As I began to grapple with adolescence, things with my mother changed. Weekends were for my friends, time at home was spent in my room, records blasting, gabbing on the telephone. I had managed to turn some of my insecurities into uniqueness, and my sadness into humor. I loved some of my classes and wrote a long US history paper on protest songs from the Vietnam War. I was obsessed with music, and was sometimes late to school if a good song came on the radio. I couldn't bear to leave it. I loaned all my clothes and borrowed everyone else's. I hung an Indian tapestry on the ceiling of my bedroom and every afternoon my little gang and I played music, snuck cigarettes, and talked about boys. Some of my friends were boarders from New York and I often went home with them on the weekends. It was clear to me that New York would be my post-high school home—and it was, for over a decade. Somehow, my ever-resilient mother adapted to everything that came her way. She became a national prize-winning teacher. She bought sleek, neutral Scandinavian furniture and redid her apartment. She read poetry, novels, and learned to cook and have dinner parties. She continued to knit beautiful things, made from spectacular and rare wool from Iceland and Scotland. She made countless baby blankets for anyone she knew who was pregnant.

The weekly Saturday excursions got better with every passing year. At some point in my early-twenties, the Saturdays together shopping and having lunch became scarcer. They usually took place in New York or Madrid, and were always special days.

Part II

Fifteen Years Later

10

I'd like to be the same woman for at least three months in a row, maybe even a year. And I'd like to have a home, some place to keep my winter coat and my books and to read in bed in.

—Martha Gellhorn, *Diaries*

I WAS IN A CAR, being driven from a small Northeastern college, where I'd given a talk to an all-white audience on African Americans who fought in the Spanish Civil War. I was on my way to another college, where I teach and live. In my talk I told the students that those young black Americans who risked—and in some cases gave—their lives in Spain in the late thirties had been neglected by history. I was moved as I said this, but I don't know if it meant anything to them. Obama was president.

My driver was proudly at the helm of a new hybrid car. He was a seemingly kind, elderly man from Poughkeepsie. He asked me if I was married. *No*, I said. Did I like to ski? *No*. The truth was, every one of his banal questions made me feel like an impostor. I needed a driver because I don't drive. This was just one of the many things that prevented me from fitting in completely to the daily life of the pastoral landscape I'd settled in.

The driver's name was Abraham, and during the long, slow ride that evening he told me he was Jewish. He had to relax quite a bit and peer back at me repeatedly through the rearview mirror before bringing that up. I told him there was a Jewish Studies program at Sheldon, my college, and we happily talked about New York delis, rugelach, mushroom barley soup, and Florida. He told jokes. He was going to retire in Florida with his brother and sister-in-law. The Northeast was too cold, he said.

I simply expressed enthusiasm for his plan. He nodded in agreement, but then said wistfully, "On the one hand there's nothing like the colors of the leaves in the fall around here. And the summers are something." "Indeed," I said. The truth was, my thoughts had nothing to do with the weather or nature. I myself was wistful because I was about to leave.

There were no other cars on the road. It was just Abraham

and me. It was dusk, and a sparkling evening, for what it's worth. I wasn't in the mood to tell him things that would undoubtedly interest him but would require hours of explanation: that only my father was Jewish, that I was raised Catholic, and that even though I sounded and looked American, my family was from Spain. I was passing, and though part of me did want to talk all about it, most of me just wanted to get home, privacy intact.

As we approached the town where I live, its green lawns gracing the campus, its pretty, Puritan, wooden houses impeccably restored by architectural historians—far from the pseudo-urbanity of Poughkeepsie—the driver kept saying that this was real countryside. He called it Hicksville, "the stix." He began to rap and rhyme in American Yiddish about Sheldon—no hustle-bustle, full of local-yokels, a rinky-dink town. "How can you live here?" he asked.

Abraham dropped me off on my empty, carefully landscaped lane—a movie set, really, *It's a Wonderful Life* meets *Nightmare on Elm Street*—in front of my looming empty house, and I wondered if he would drive straight back. I drew all the blinds and was afraid to peek out to see if he was still there, parked with his lights off, a testament to my phony conversation, to loneliness in rural America, to everything that was wrong with my life. He was gone. I saw bats flying around in the dusk.

The spring semester was almost over. Soon I would be leaving on sabbatical, returning once again to Spain. As I got ready for bed I remembered what it was like when I first arrived in this New England town. One particular moment stood out. It was noon on a sunny fall day, not a week after the September 11 attacks, and I couldn't quite believe I had left New York. I was once again in a small town, this time on an isolated, pristine campus in western

Massachusetts. A gentle wind was blowing the first fallen leaves around the lawns and the knobby paved walkways linking one stately colonial-style college building to another.

I had just finished my first or second week of teaching, my new job. I was proud to be there, and exhausted from smiling, from trying to learn everything I could about an author before daring to mention their name in front of confident students. It was still warm, and the classrooms and my small office were in a particularly old building, a converted fraternity house called Cabot Hall. I quickly learned that I would hear details of campus history over and over—"The Sheldon Inn used to be over there on South Street"—and that any nugget of information could be a conversation piece in this small town.

I bought a bicycle, because I imagined myself commuting to work, gliding down the hill from my faculty apartment like an Oxford don. Obviously, I forgot to think of the snow.

A bestselling book had just come out about a professor in a small New England college town, and though the town was called Athena in the novel, everyone knew it was based on Sheldon, where the author had been a writer-in-residence for a year back in the sixties. One of the secondary characters was a French professor who was the young chair of the Modern Languages department. As I read the novel I identified and imagined her working in my office.

When I went running in the area I rarely saw anybody. People occasionally asked, "Do you like living here?" I was never sure that I knew what "living here" meant. I suspected the question came with an implied assumption that I did not like living here, and that I especially didn't like living here because I had moved from New York and had a foreign name. But the truth is that I fell in love with the town and the campus from the first time I saw them. They were beautiful. They reminded me of the Vermont of my childhood, and I felt safe there.

After my sabbatical I would no longer be allowed to stay in the faculty housing. I had decided to look for a house to buy. A house for one person. That was not as easy as it sounds. At first, the thought of an actual "house" seemed too complicated for me. But the only apartment option within walking distance was an old mill that was being renovated—very slowly. All the windows were still broken, and the floors were covered with debris. I walked through the halls and projected "units" one day, and it was like being on a movie set for a crack house. When the real estate agent began describing the great common areas they were going to build on each floor, I told him that maybe we should go see the pretty Cape I had initially turned down. He said it had been taken off the market, but he would email me if it came up for sale again while I was away. I knew I wouldn't be good at buying a house. It could wait until after my sabbatical.

I had plans, tickets, and funding for a year's research. I had a prestigious fellowship. I had a new passport. In the closet where I kept my suitcases I found a box filled with my first books. My favorite was a vintage, indeed antique, book from the 1940s called *The Little Spanish Dancer*. Who gave me this book? Perhaps my mother found it at a yard sale? Later in life I took flamenco lessons for years. Was I that basic? Was it because of this forgotten book? Next to the box, my old doll's house rested on the floor. It seemed to echo the house I was standing in.

I was going to Spain. I looked in the fridge and saw the expiration date on the milk, far beyond my date of departure. It made me sad. I felt like a traitor. I hated expiration dates. I realized once again that I was not sure why I was going for such a long time and that I was rather frightened by the idea. Yes, I had a research project, and I was supposed to write a biography. All of it was official. And I was going to see my mother. These were plans I had made carefully.

I took a car service to the airport. At first I felt relieved to be there, but as soon as I realized I was leaving for so long I started to cry. I was overwhelmed with a feeling of alienation. I made a spectacle of myself among the garishly lit souvenir shops and pretzel carts at the provincial airport. How could I cry in Albany, of all places? Had it come to that?

I'd flown between the US and Spain at least a hundred times, and every time I got to the airport it reminded me that I was apparently born to go back and forth, no matter how permanently I tried to settle in one place or the other. I went outside the terminal and smoked two cigarettes and called a friend in New York but got her voicemail.

I was a historian, and I loved teaching. I had a secure job. My mother was finally back in Spain, as she had always wanted to be. My father was long dead, and thus he could no longer actively offend me by his terrible silence. And yet. My latest relationship had not worked out, and I could not envision my future during or beyond the sabbatical. Not at all. Living in New England alone? Was I really Spanish? European? Did it matter?

11

Deborah Levy
Deborah Levy
PRESTON
UN PUEBLO TRAICIONADO
El expediente de mi madre
MUJERES PARA LA HISTORIA
DUVEEN
MERYLE SECREST
AMERICAN DIRT
Robert Hughes
Barcelona
COHEN
Bella del Señor

I TOOK A TAXI TO my mother's house in Madrid around ten the following morning. Some people had large groups of family and friends waiting for them at Barajas who received them with kisses and signs, and even balloons, but not me. My mother had been waiting for me impatiently at home. I knew from experience she had been awake for hours, periodically peering out the window of her 1950s brick apartment building, "just in case." This building was the most recent incarnation of the downsizing that had beset our family's former grandeur in Spain. The history of my family was one of shrinkage: financial, residential, and biological. My grandparents and great-grandparents had had estates on Mallorca and private townhouses in Madrid near the Prado Museum. The women had their clothes made at Fortuny, and Worth in Paris. The men had tailors in London.

We had lost the original apartment that my mother, and later I, intermittently, grew up in years before, and my grandfather and aunt had moved into what was now my mother's place. Both of them were my homes, the only semi-permanent places there had been in my life. After three decades of living and working in the United States, my mother had finally made it back to Spain and stayed. The landscaping around the building made me happy: palm trees, cacti, and hydrangeas. Its dry southern air calmed me.

I was greeted by Concha, who looked after my mother and was from Extremadura, who gave me kisses and a big smile. She was in her early sixties, and had been a beauty in her time. She was still impeccably turned out, even to come work at our house. She looked a hundred times better than most of the *señoras* she had worked for. And she had raised three children on her own. Yet the most amazing thing about her—which I remembered each time I arrived from the States and then forgot as I got used to Spain and its paradoxes—was that she was illiterate. How she managed, I had no idea. She'd only confirmed this twice. The first time when we tried to give her a shopping list, and the second while lamenting that she had no man in her life and that internet dating was off-limits to her because she couldn't read or write. She left her husband years ago for the owner of bar, but then he had left her, and her husband wouldn't have her back.

Concha stepped aside and there was my mother, waiting. She had a debilitating neuromuscular disease, which had appeared out of the blue when she was sixty and forced her to retire early. She was physically fragile now, but ever beautiful with her dark hair and sparkling eyes, and her mind was sharper than ever. I embraced her and we both began to cry, and then to laugh at the fact that we were crying. Here she was, the same woman who had been an independent young mother in New England and who played with me in the snow. This was the body that went with the voice I spoke to every day long distance. Here she was with her books, and her friendships from her youth recovered. Clearly she was very much at home again in Madrid, but what about me? Where was I supposed to live in the long term?

I was to stay at my mother's during my sabbatical. In my old room, in my old neighborhood. I hadn't really thought this through, but I wanted to go home, somehow, and this was it.

My room was full of storage boxes, and I barely had space for my ridiculously huge American suitcases. I slept for a couple of days and started to work on what would become a biography of Consuelo Marqués, an incredible woman who had taken part in the anti-Fascist fight during the Spanish Civil War. I was professionally based, through the fellowship, at a research center on the outskirts of the city. It was a haul on the metro to get there, but I got along well with one or two colleagues, and they had a great library. It was called the Tomás Navarro Tomás library, and as I often had overdue books, the palindromic name popped up in my inbox with frequent and annoying reminders. I had zero curiosity about the library's name, even though I knew it was familiar. I just couldn't be bothered to place it.

Living in Spain full-time again, for the first time since I was fifteen, overwhelmed me with cultural changes, facts and names and contexts that had seemed dim and distant to me from the United States. A colleague had just sent me a fascinating new book on the brutal Franco repression in Sevilla. The campaign there against the Republicans had been led by a fearsome general, Queipo de Llano. I left this book on the big marble table in my mother's living room, thinking she might be curious about it. There was a photograph of the Queipo on the cover. But when I pointed it out to her, thinking she would be interested in a new Spanish Civil War book, she simply turned the book over so that the photo faced downward.

Was it the subject of the war that she was tired of? Was it Sevilla and the war? After all, the book hit on the time and place of her birth. I hadn't thought of that. The subjects I studied and taught were the life she had experienced, but we had never spoken about these things. I realized that the book had stirred up difficult memories for her.

"Why were you born in Sevilla?" I asked her one day, realizing how one can go through years of life without knowing the most basic things about one's background. Though my grandfather was originally from Mallorca, and my grandmother from Barcelona, our family had lived in Madrid for over half a century before her birth. Sevilla was in far off Andalucía. "Because of the war," she said. How little I knew about fundamental parts of her life. She had taught the Spanish Civil War in her classes at Middleton in the United States, and her bookshelves were crammed with volumes on the subject, in French, Spanish, and English. When I was little the subject of the war was amazingly well concealed in my family. Nobody in my grandfather's house ever brought it up. I never associated the grim history with my family members. With her reaction to the book with Queipo de Llano on its cover, I realized how much information I was missing. In fact, almost everything was missing. I had heard her say she was born in a boardinghouse, but both her parents were from well off families. They had grown up in splendid homes in Madrid and Barcelona. Why were they displaced and homeless, in makeshift housing in Sevilla in December 1937? Geographically, this made no sense. It was clearly a political itinerary.

I needed to know. How could I be a specialist in twentieth-century Spain when I didn't even know my own history? What had really become of my mother's family, or my father's? How would I ever figure out who I was without knowing my family's past? Was I an integral part of this Spanish history, or some kind of postmodern American observer? Why so much secrecy? How bad could it all be?

It took no small degree of coaxing to get her to talk about it, but I kept insisting, until one day she called me into her room and told me all she could remember about those years. About her life. She was sitting up in her beautiful nineteenth-century French bed with inlaid marquetry of pastoral scenes: damsels and gentlemen walking in the countryside under the shade of luscious trees. Fairytale images, so far from what I was about to hear. I was perched on a tiny, equally old but newly reupholstered toile chair.

Her mother, my grandmother Marieta, died decades before I was born. She had been beautiful. She studied at the Sacré Coeur in Paris and attended a finishing school in Switzerland. She was the only daughter of a Galician aristocrat and a family of Catalan industrialists with headquarters in Barcelona and England. She had two brothers who died tragically. She met my grandfather, who was fifteen years older, at a society wedding in Barcelona. What he didn't know when they married was that she was already very ill. She had tuberculosis of the kidneys and had spent long, secret periods at sanatoriums. Her parents, who cherished their only girl, never told her just how serious it was, though the pain and weakness it caused must have given her an idea.

My grandfather was part of a political family. His father's brother was a longstanding leader, and my grandfather launched his own career during the Republic in the early 1930s. Their wedding took place in Barcelona, they spent their honeymoon in Morocco, and then they moved into their large Madrid apartment. But the war soon interrupted their lives.

My grandparents were in Barcelona when the Civil War broke out. In the chaos of the early days, my grandfather and one of his young brothers-in-law were out walking when they were detained by anarchists who had taken control of the streets in response to the military uprising. The two men were taken to a prison and interrogated. My grandfather explained that he was an anti-uprising Republican, but they didn't believe him, dressed in his posh clothes with his wealthy industrialist brother-in-law in tow. They were held overnight, and the next morning a young anarchist shoeshine boy, who knew my grandfather and had heard about the arrests, went to the prison to beg that they release him. He swore to the guards that my grandfather was "on our side." One of the guards reluctantly told my grandfather he could go, and my grandfather said he would only leave if his brother-in-law, sitting right next to him, was released as well. The guard smiled, and asked my grandfather to hand over a small gun he was carrying for safety. The guard played with it for a few seconds, then held it to my great-uncle's head and shot him point blank. He pointed the gun at my grandfather and said, "Get out of here, now. You are free, but this will teach you to think more carefully about who you hang out with." I don't know how my grandfather broke the news to his young bride that her brother had just been executed with his own gun. The body, along with many others, was removed from the prison and dumped in a ditch off a main road. My great-grandmother searched for her son's body night and day. There was an article—we have the yellowed newspaper clipping in a folder—written about her tireless mission to find him. She was finally able to bury her son.

The arrest and the execution had been warnings, and my grandfather no longer felt safe. He hid out at my grandmother's dressmaker's for as long as he could. He was finally able to buy a ticket on a boat going to Genoa. He was turned away at the Italian port and was forced to go back to Spain, penniless and barefoot. By then he learned that his wife, Marieta, was pregnant with their first daughter, my mother, Odilia. This is when he also discovered just how sick she was. He had to find a way to protect her. Through family connections, he managed to be sent to Sevilla.

My pregnant grandmother joined him there, where they lived in a boardinghouse. There were other prominent Catalan families taking refuge there, including one of my grandfather's closest friends. In the meantime, their beautiful apartment in Madrid, where they had barely lived a moment together, was ransacked. Everything had been stolen or destroyed, jewels taken and hocked, furniture axed to bits for firewood. Thus it was that my mother was born in the rented room in Sevilla on a winter's day during the war. She was three months premature, and the doctor left her for dead out of my grandmother's sight, until her infant screams and wails proved him wrong. My grandmother's health deteriorated as the war progressed, yet she became pregnant again right after the war's end. In 1940, my aunt Inés was born. Less than a year later, my grandmother was dead at the age of thirty-three. Her surviving brother had fought with the military rebels, in part to avenge his brother's murder. He was shot in action, and after an operation was given large amounts of morphine. He became an addict, spending the few remaining years of his short life in and out of hospitals. Because of the war, my maternal great-grandparents lost all three of their children within five years of each other.

They had their doorman hide all their china in the water tower of their apartment building in Barcelona, and to this day my mother and I have copious sets of French china, with settings for fifty people, that survived the war without a chink. We don't use them, but we can't let them go. They were last used for my grandparents' wedding lunch and are now all packed in recycled boxes from El Corte Inglés. They are in my bedroom now, because our storage unit has some kind of unsolvable humidity issue. Though she can barely use her hands or write anymore, my mother repacked all of the china carefully and labeled the boxes. LIMOGES. BLUE LIMOGES. CHAMPAGNE. PORCELAIN, TIGERS, AND NYMPHS. Nearly a hundred years later we are still guarding the china and the champagne and cordial glasses. It's all that's left of the splendor my grandmother and her family had known in Barcelona—those objects, and photos of my grandmother, especially one on which she had written to her daughters, "*A mis nenas, Mamá.*"

After she died, my mother and her sister grew up with my grandfather in the looted Madrid apartment under the care of a succession of nannies.

I thought of my mother and her baby sister as motherless orphans with an aging father in the bleak postwar. My mother's earliest memories are of her mother being very ill. She remembers flying alone to Barcelona with her in 1940 so that she could have an operation. My mother was nearly three years old, and was very excited about being on a plane and that the stewardesses passed out glasses of water. During her recovery from surgery, my grandmother taught my mother songs, and was still very beautiful. She chain-smoked, using a long cigarette holder. She died on November 2, 1941.

My mother was sent, almost immediately, to the British school in Madrid. It was a small coed school, with about eighty students. It was exceptional. It wasn't Catholic, and there were no uniforms. The children played, learned English, and had their own orchestra, which was directed by a little boy. They put on plays, and my grandfather went to see the performances. The two years she spent there were a happy time for my mother, but my grandfather's stern sisters soon intervened, and she was forced to transfer to an all-girls Catholic nun's school. This was when she really started to miss her mother the most.

Once a year, my mother and Inés's grandparents visited from Barcelona. They lived to see their only granddaughters, the vital connection to their deceased daughter. Their visits were brief and far between because my grandfather never forgave them for "hiding" their daughter's illness from him. They stayed at the Palace Hotel. The two girls loved riding up and down in the elevator, spotting glamorous guests, and trying on all their grandmother's jewels, hats, and nightgowns. When they were older they traveled to Barcelona often, especially Odilia.

My grandfather was seldom around. He went to work and the girls went to school, six days a week, including Saturdays. He spent his weekends in the countryside, or on archeological digs. Thousands of people adjusted their politics during the war in order to survive, but because of his family name it was harder for him to live under the radar. He had been a high-profile conservative Republican before the war, and because of this he was kept down in the repressive postwar years. As late as the1970s there were stores on the Calle Serrano in Madrid that he would not go to, because in the 1940s the shopkeepers had called him a "*rojo.*" I could think of few things more ridiculous than my grandfather being a political extremist, but the war had polarized people and baseless judgements lived on. The more I learned about my family, the better I understood why there had been so much silence, and so much bitterness, and so many secrets.

In June my research project took me to Sevilla. After a day of poring over archives and having dinner in the Barrio Santa Cruz, I called my mother to ask her for the name of the boardinghouse where she had been born over seven decades before. I wasn't confident she would remember. But of course she did. "Otte. Pensión Otte," she said immediately. The last thing I expected was that the boardinghouse would have a German name.

I looked at old newspapers online and found some ads for the defunct pensión and a postcard. The postcard showed a beautiful *sevillana* villa. Lush trees shaded the building. The ad proclaimed, "Comfortable hotel. Excellent food. Modest prices." The neighborhood was auspiciously called "El Porvenir," "The Future," although another way of translating it that conveys an additional resonance would be "What Is to Come."

I looked into it further and discovered that the owner was a woman, and it turned out she was Jewish, and had married a non-Jewish German. By the mid-1930s she was a widow, and had clearly been able to pass as a German in the Spain of that era, hence the success of her pensión in the heart of a German neighborhood in the middle of the Spanish Civil War in a city that was controlled by Franco with his Nazi and Italian allies.

Her son, Enrique Otte, as an adolescent may have shared meals with my grandfather, or remarked what a cute baby my mother was. Though, of course, these are my own musings. He had an intriguing, wandering life worthy of a W. G. Sebald novel. Born in Madrid in 1923, he went to study in Germany and managed to survive there between 1939 and 1944. He was never suspected of being part Jewish and was, in fact, drafted by the German army in 1944. He escaped this fate thanks to his Spanish nationality, which he had adopted when he was twenty-one. He returned to postwar Spain briefly, but soon left for England, where he spent two years, then went back to Germany, where he studied philosophy for another two. He eventually came back to the *barrio*, "El Porvenir" in Sevilla, in 1948.

His mother's Pensión Otte continued to thrive throughout the postwar years, and many famous guests stayed there: the writers Marguerite Yourcenar and Henry Miller, the historian Hugh Trevor-Roper. Enrique Otte, who had studied history, was unable to find a job in Spain and finally went back to Berlin again in 1966, where he secured a professorship in Latin American history at the Free University. He was a brilliant historian and spent the remaining forty years of his life writing about the economic, banking, and historical ties between Spain and the Caribbean in the sixteenth century. He did pioneering research in the Archivo de Indias in Sevilla and published many studies, including a volume of collected letters sent by Spaniards who had sought their fortune in the New World to their families back in Spain. The letters show an intimate side of history, revealing the loneliness and homesickness of the travelers. Distances were immense in the 1500s, the voyages were often one-way, and transatlantic correspondence among people who could not read or write was a challenge. The uniform style of the letters suggests a professional writer was on hand for the illiterate or semi-literate émigrés, yet the missives differ in the personal details and situations of their authors. This one, from Juan de Escobar to his daughter Ana de Escobar, is addressed to "My desired daughter, in the passageway of San Pablo, in the parish of the Magdalena, in Sevilla."

Jamaica, 1. IV. 1567
Desired daughter:

Many days have passed since I wrote you many letters sent by many means, as I have also written to relatives and friends to see if you are dead or alive. About a year ago, a clergyman left this island, and when said clergyman arrived in Spain he knew you were alive, and he sent me a message to that effect by way of Santo Domingo. I implore you, if you are married and your husband is inclined to bring you to these parts, please come because all I have will be for you and your husband, because I do not dare travel to Spain as I am always ill, and I don't want to die on the sea, and if God brought you here I would be greatly consoled by the sight of you, and I might even regain my health. I would pay whoever brought you for all the expenses and costs you might incur on the journey, wherever you might land. May our Lord give you the health that I wish I had myself. The date on the island of Jamaica is the first of April in 1567. I await your orders.

Juan de Escobar

The Pensión Otte, Enrique Otte, and the letters from abroad all made a strong impression on me. They represented a history of transience, displacement, and the struggle for stability and home. I was surprised to find myself sympathetic to the plight of a colonial adventurer.

My mother's family had always come closest to representing permanence to me, even though I thought my mother and I had been largely deprived of it. But the more I learned about the specific circumstances of my parents' respective families during the war, the more I realized that by comparison, my own dislocated life had been a model of peace and security. There had been no soldiers, no Nazis.

And yet I also sensed I had inherited some kind of perpetuation of the Spanish Civil War and of the values imposed by Franco, especially those that had constrained my mother. She left Spain in 1968, like Enrique Otte had left in the 1930s and 1940s, like Juan de Escobar had left in the sixteenth century. Like them, she left to seek a better life. I was to learn that my father left Madrid in the 1950s, and also would have liked to return to Spain to die, like Juan de Escobar. Different times, different motives, but the forces—of poverty in the case of Escobar, and social repression in the cases of my mother, father, and Enrique Otte—had been strong enough for them to abandon their homes and families.

12

BEFORE COMING TO SPAIN, before my sabbatical, I started therapy. I had first gone in the late summer after I moved from New York to Sheldon. In July, just before, I had been in Madrid, and learned that my aunt Inés had lung cancer that had metastasized everywhere. I did not know how to tell my mother, who had also been seeing doctors but was still teaching in America. For close to two years, she had difficulty going up stairs and had started falling unexpectedly. Just as Inés's diagnosis was confirmed, my mother had a muscle biopsy and was told she had an untreatable degenerative neuromuscular disease. Finally, she knew why everything had become so difficult. Every muscle in her arms, legs, and throat was in the process of atrophying.

Despite her own intensifying weakness, my mother took a leave from her teaching to go to Spain and look after her sister. Because Inés had never married, she had taken care of my grandfather when his health seriously deteriorated. He lived to be eighty-six. Now she, just shy of sixty, was dying. She was in great pain, and they operated on her back when they shouldn't have because the cancer was everywhere, and it only made her last few months an inferno. I couldn't take time off because my job was new. The last time I spoke to *tía* Inés was by phone. Like everyone in the world she had just seen—from her hospital bed—the images of the September 11 attacks in New York, where she had come to visit me while I was a graduate student. We hadn't told her just how bad her situation was. By phone from Sheldon, I tried to sound upbeat and said I would see her at Christmas. But she knew I was lying. "Nena," she said, using her nickname for me, "I won't make it that long. What I have is like *las torres gemelas* (the Twin Towers)." I knew exactly what she meant. When we saw one plane fly into the Twin Towers, we wondered and worried. When we saw the second plane, and the buildings collapsed, that was it. And it all happened so fast. Now she herself was disintegrating, and there was no way to stop or hide it. She also said she didn't want me to see her "like that." I didn't yet know what she meant.

The doctor gave Inés six months, and so it was, to the day. On December 24, I was on a plane to Madrid. The city was rainy and cold when I arrived the next morning, and the hospital smelled of disinfectant.

I rushed to the room number I had been given. My mother was sitting on a pleather armchair where she had been sleeping for over three weeks, inseparable from the once baby sister whom she would have to bury. In the time it had taken me to go through customs and find a taxi to the hospital, my aunt had died, minutes before I arrived. The body I saw in the hospital bed was not Inés. There was nothing about this figure that I could recognize as my aunt, my "auntie," as she signed all her letters to me, acknowledging my American side. My mother said, "Hold her hand."

Feli the cook, family, and friends came to the wake and the burial. It rained continuously. Inés was buried in the family grave with her grandparents and my grandfather and his siblings. There was nowhere to engrave her name on the front of the tombstone, so it had to be squashed onto the side. Feli grabbed a handful of damp earth and tossed it into the grave. I wanted to do the same, but I didn't dare. Nobody had told me about this, and I didn't have her confidence, her connection to the earth or to death. She had been like a surrogate mother to my aunt.

Amid the heartache and gloom, I had been somehow heartened to learn that we had a family tomb. Not quite a mausoleum, but a collective spot. I mentioned to my mother that at least we could all be buried together. My mother said, "Well, we've actually just been informed of something: there is only room for one more." Part of me started to wonder, where was I going to be buried? When I mentioned this to my therapist, he said, "Why don't you cross that bridge when you come to it?" Of course, that made sense. And yet.

Inés's funeral mass was held at the Convent of Las Descalzas, originally built in 1559 as a palace for Emperor Charles V. I was transfixed by the exquisite singing of the cloistered nuns hidden behind intricate wooden screens. It was fascinating to me that these nuns should still exist, and that only a very few people were allowed to see them. After many years at the Royal Palace, Inés had been transferred—at her request—to work at this convent, which also belonged to Spain's Patrimonio Nacional, the organization that protects places of unique cultural value. Inés had grown close to the nuns, who often gave her lemons and other treats from their gardens. They had insisted on singing and organizing her farewell with my mother, as if Inés were a sister they were also losing. Inés had called the sisters "*mis monjitas*," and they filled the church with flowers and special relics, highly polished pieces of silver and other treasures they had. Along with our family and friends, dozens of Inés's colleagues from the Patrimonio Nacional were present, including higher-ups, electricians, and plumbers.

After Inés's death my mother stayed, permanently, in the family home in Madrid. I eventually moved her things out of her house near Boston. She only wanted her books. I kept trying to send her other things, but she didn't want anything from all her years in America. Not a button.

With Inés gone, and my mother ill and living in Spain, I felt very impoverished and fragile in terms of my already very small family. Inés had always been in Madrid, my mother had lived near Boston, and now Inés was nowhere, and my mother was far away. When I had taken the job in Sheldon, I thought it would be nice to live a couple of hours from my mother.

That's when I started to see Dr. Cohen, who I now continued speaking to via phone sessions from Madrid. He had been sympathetic when my aunt died and when my mother was diagnosed, and I hoped he could help me find a way to rebuild my life on my own now.

He said that the change the sabbatical would bring, the chance to be on my own in a new place, would help me find myself. It sounded vaguely promising. I pretended to listen to this, the same way I've always pretended to meditate in yoga class, evincing an earnest expression while privately rolling my eyes with all the maturity of a fourteen-year-old. As soon as I hear "Close your eyes and take a deep breath," I sneak them open and pretty much stop breathing until everyone else has opened theirs. Dr. Cohen thought I should embrace being alone and avoid romantic relationships until I had done more "work" on myself. Since I had recently broken up with Alex, my boyfriend from graduate school, I had developed a few crushes here and there but I hadn't fallen in love. This was my goal. Alex and I had lived together in New York. But since, I had moved to Sheldon, and he had moved to Los Angeles to become a screenwriter. He had urged me to move with him, and to break with my past and try something new. My own professional life, and my desire to live closer to Europe weren't really issues for him. I understood. We wanted different things.

Who can compete with Hollywood? But the timing seemed terrible to me. Cohen suggested that once I did my time *alone*, I would be ready for a caring, healthy, trusting, mature relationship. This sounded nice, but highly unrealistic to me. At the beginning I was glad to have someone so sympathetic and interested in my life. Then I grew skeptical. Then I forgot to think about it. He told me, in any case, I had to accept that I would probably not meet anyone in a real-life situation, and that I would have to face the online dating world. I didn't want to believe this.

Cohen asked if I was writing my novel, which was something I had told him I wanted to do once I got my life sorted. "No," I said, "you of all people should know I'm not writing. I'm busy trying to 'find myself.'"

"Well, you should write," he said. "It's what you say you want to do. Plus, you're never going to have a novel if you don't write."

"I'm trying to quit smoking, and I'm learning to be alone. With my mother."

He was relentless.

"Are you running or doing some other kind of exercise? Anyway, you've got to start writing your novel."

Easy for him to say.

The novel, I told myself, was a figment of my imagination. I started it and rued the day because it seemed unlikely I would ever finish it. How could I possibly work on a novel when I was questioning who I was, where my life was going, and I had a biography to write and a ton of academic deadlines ahead of me? Plus, who ever told me I could write a novel? Nobody ever told me I *couldn't*, but nobody ever asked me to either. I had written personal pieces and poems, but they were short and scrappy and ended up in liquor store boxes at the bottom of closets in rental apartments. I took creative writing classes in college, but only once, while in graduate school in New York, did I pluck up the courage to submit a personal piece about—what else?—my parents. I was chosen to read it at a conference on memoir. My mother and friends came to hear me, and the auditorium was packed. It was exciting, yet after that, I crawled back into my shell and only wrote scholarly pieces. A novel, at least my first one, as I saw it, would have to be somewhat personal and that would inevitably betray my background, because I had been raised to value privacy and discretion above all else.

I thought about this conundrum often when I went running through the Retiro Park. My problems didn't go away when I ran, but they diminished considerably and were put in perspective. As I sped along tree-lined promenades and grassy hills, I saw old people sitting on benches, parents with their children—some of them very little, in prams, some already grown up, some with Down's syndrome, some in wheelchairs. I saw young lovers and illicit couples enjoying the anonymity of the city's public spaces. The park was a refuge for those who needed respite from the hard business of the city streets. Including me. This was the same park where I used to play on the swings and the dusty ground.

At night I watched all the Woody Allen DVDs I found at my mother's and bought more. This was pre-streaming. Purchasing them required a long walk along the Calle Claudio Coello to the Corte Inglés, that vast bunker of a department store that had been the object of my consumerist daydreams for years. I found two box sets and made my choice and wended my way to a register through aisles lined with video games—I'm not even sure they were still called that. Then I went to buy some new bed linens. It was so cozy to have new crisp blue-and-white striped cotton sheets and watch old movies.

What was to become of my future? How was I going to do the research for my biography, write a novel, or reconnect to my past when I felt my life was at a crossroads? I loved Madrid, but it felt unusual to be there for an extended period of time. I also had only a few close friends in Madrid at that point. One of my oldest friends from New York insisted via email that I forget about living, and just write.

And Cohen's favorite topic was loneliness. "Why are you so afraid of being alone?" My answer was always the same: "Isn't everyone afraid of being alone? Look at all those desperate people out there trying to find someone. It's not that weird!" Did I mention I am an only child?

His prescription for me was to plunge into my fear headfirst, and live like Emerson or Thoreau, albeit in an urban Spanish setting with my mother and Concha, reflecting deeply on my fears, meditating, cultivating my independence. To make him happy, I pretended that this was my goal. It all sounded distantly appealing but impossibly vague, like "making a billion dollars." I knew some people did it, but it was not in the cards for me. And there was a legion of enemies determined to foil his plan, a plan I was going to resist anyway.

My female friends and even mere acquaintances all seemed to have a potential paramour up their sleeve who would be "perfect" for me. I told a couple of Spanish friends about my shrink's recommendation and they looked alarmed. In Spain there was nothing worse than being alone—it was tantamount to being a leper. "Why would he want you to suffer so? Life is so hard alone, so lonely," said my old friend Mónica. The few people who seemed to agree with Cohen all repeated that infamous Spanish proverb to me: "*Mejor sola que mal acompañada.*" Better to be alone than in bad company. But the truth was that for me—and I finally understood this—this proverb was more of a posteriori consolation, something to be said to someone who's been abandoned, than an a priori recommendation.

There was also an insurmountable cultural and gender barrier between Cohen and me that I never got past. The fact that I was bicultural, and bilingual, was never considered. Because my current life in Spain—and so many memories—unfolded in Spanish, I wasn't just telling him things; I was translating everything. To him, Spain was a sunny resort that I was lucky to visit frequently. Good wines, beautiful landscapes. All true. When we talked in the winter, he complained about the multiple snowstorms in New England. Had I taken a sabbatical to come to Spain to hear about local blizzards in Sheldon from a therapist? On the other hand, he gave excellent advice if I had a specific conundrum, which I sometimes did.

Katya, my Italian-Russian friend from college, was living in Switzerland with her wealthy Spanish tycoon husband. She had all kinds of theories about men and about my life. I only ever saw her fleetingly because they traveled to attend parties, operas, and art openings. It was a full-time job.

She called me from their many houses and we had lengthy conversations. She gave me confidence, because I knew she didn't like to waste her time, so I figured she thought I was a worthy investment. We were an odd phone-friend couple. She in their Swiss mansion or the Marbella villa, and me in my newly recovered teenage room.

The irony was that Katya was the granddaughter of famous

Italian communists who had lived in Russia. She had always been beautiful, and her guest lists included arcane royalty and people famous just for being famous. I could have sworn she'd also become taller, but it may have been that she never wore heels before. She was my age but treated me with an older sister attitude. She was very entertaining. Her Spanish had a Russian accent but was fluent and peppered with expressions from her grandmother that gave her conversation a folksy edge. Of a mutual friend, Antonio, who was a bit of a pro with tricks up his sleeve, she said, "*Tiene más conchas que los Galápagos.*" He has more shells than the Galapagos turtles. My mother used many of the same expressions. One day I heard the Galapagos line three times. I was obviously way behind on life lessons because it took me a while, alone, just to figure out what the expression meant, let alone how to apply its wisdom to my life. Shells are hard, people are tough. I got it. They'll run circles around me. But knowing it didn't make me any tougher. Katya summed me up: "You know what your problem is? You're a romantic." This was clearly worse even than being a decadent bourgeois.

The months went by. It would be impossible for me, she admonished on a call from Lausanne, to find a new man. Impossible. First of all, because I worked too hard, always doing research and writing, which she disapproved of as she saw no clear reward to what I did, certainly no great money. She saw me as a small-time romantic. But second of all, she explained, even if I devoted myself to nothing but the pursuit of the male species, there were no men to be had. She was the prime evidence of her argument, a beautiful, intelligent, exceptionally well-educated, multilingual woman. It took her many years to find the ideal man, with unhappiness along the way. She had a theory, many theories, such as that 20 percent of men were psychopaths, 20 percent were womanizers, the other 20 percent were alcoholics, the other 20 percent were gay, and the other 50 percent were married. The womanizers—the most fun and hence the most dangerous—she divided into Don Juans (bad, they hate women) and Casanovas (good, they wanted to give you pleasure while it lasted which would not be long).

However, all this convincing but fuzzy math did not stop her from energetically reviewing in detail the few men we knew in common, all of whose foibles she had sussed out as if she were the author of a neo-medieval treatise on humors. They were all to be avoided. Pierre-Yves, a historian, was single but had grown sad and stingy. Eduardo, who was quite brilliant, had three strikes against him: he was anxious, anxious, anxious. What about James, I asked? He was a longtime Irish expat in Madrid who I'd taken a shine to. She said he was the type who might never settle down, and who somehow managed to survive in Spain cobbling together documentary films. She said he was probably a commitment-phobe, and would meet someone else and I would be covered with horns—the Spanish expression for cheating on someone is to *ponerle los cuernos*, put horns on them. When she said this, I immediately pictured myself quite literally covered in horns, at least all around my face and head, and I shivered. "Not a nice image, is it," she said. "No!" I agreed. I did wonder if she wasn't giving James a fair shake because she knew I was interested. And yet. She spoke so confidently. Then there was Dmitri, the young Russian researcher she knew much better than I did, who seemed to have it all, and I brightened up. She sang his praises: he was hardworking, forward-looking, intelligent, healthy, resourceful, clean, tidy, and a fabulous cook. Encouraged by this break in her bleak outlook, I said, "Well, sounds like he would make a nice husband for someone." "*Sure*," she said, laughing, "a Russian researcher! Ha! A nice husband if you want to starve to death." I have never been to Moscow, but I could imagine being cold and hungry in a dingy flat. Perhaps Cohen would get his way after all, and I would be forced into solitude and be like Emily Dickinson: out with lanterns looking for myself.

Katya had particular scorn for a young American historian she had recently had lunch with. A self-professed Marxist, he attacked her for being a traitor to "the cause," for having married a wealthy man. And, she said, "He thinks he's a Communist!" She snorted with laughter. "He's never even been to a Communist country. The nerve of this guy," she said, "He's American. I was raised in the Soviet Union and *he* wanted to tell *me* about it." I thought about what Katya said: what did he know about Communism? And what did I know? I had one Soviet-bred friend, and she was certainly went against any type I could have imagined.

There were, however, two men in Marbella she thought I should meet. One, according to her, was a "merry widower" (her term) and the other some kind of northern Italian aristocrat. "A duke?" I asked. "More like a marquis," she answered. "And stop asking questions. The problem with you," she told me, "is that you take everything too seriously. And you're too picky."

I often concluded these phone conversations dizzy from the parade of abstract disqualified men, making my way along the few blocks that separated my mother's apartment from the pool. For the first time in many years I didn't have a boyfriend to plan a summer holiday with. I went to the pool as often as possible. Katya was right in that I worked too hard, but I was also extremely good at doing nothing at all, particularly if it was in the sun. I didn't even swim at the pool—I just climbed the stairs to this giant concrete slab optimistically called the "solarium" where dozens of dyed-blonde, topless females of all ages and shapes spent day after day baking themselves to a leather-like crisp.

The pool club was quite expensive, but like so many institutions in Spain it was shabby and built in a neo-fascist style, something just a notch above a YMCA, but in an outdoor post-Franco setting. I'd been going there since I was twelve, but I had never clocked as many hours as I did that summer. I used to go with my aunt Inés. Being there brought back nice memories. Now I went alone, almost every day. I set up a little desert island around my lounge chair. Now it was time to turn on my back, now it was getting too hot and time for a cool shower.

When I finished the chapter of the book I was reading, I ate an apple. I normally don't like lunch, but some days I went down to the garden cafeteria, with its plastic chairs and tables, and had gazpacho and a grilled baby sole or trout. Back at the solarium I read, played music, or listened to the housewives chattering around me. I stared up at the tops of the Mediterranean pines and pretended I was in Mallorca or Ibiza. I didn't get one iota closer to finding myself, but I did get very tan, and that was better than nothing.

Most of the women at the pool covered themselves in sunscreen-free Nivea that looked exactly like Crisco. It even came in a Crisco-shaped tin. After days of careful observation, I began to suspect that it *was* Crisco, with a little perfume added. I used a cream with a protection factor of 6 and felt like a neurotic hypochondriac. I had my doubts, because the truth was, these women looked much better than me. In America, sophisticates waxed nostalgic about the carefree reckless days depicted in the *Thin Man* movies—martinis all day and cigarettes galore. The closest thing to this in western Europe is probably Spain.

The pool women baked all day, anointing their bodies with one hand and smoking with the other. The solarium floor was studded with terracotta ashtrays overflowing with cigarette butts. Some used their empty Nivea tins as ashtrays.

On the days that I skipped lunch there was an interlude of silent bliss for me starting at around 1:30 p.m. when they went downstairs to have a beer, wine, or vermouth with a two-course lunch, then came back upstairs around 3:00 p.m. to sleep it off. Some Spaniards have perfected the art of pure denial. I often heard someone complaining, while smoking, about a sore throat, blaming the symptom on a draft in their bedroom the night before, or the air conditioning at a department store or cinema. Instantly someone would chime in that there was a bug going around, someone else would agree, and all of them would nod together while puffing away in sympathy at the perils of modern life. Though I saw through this denial, it made me envious. I smoked too, and I wished that I was not bicultural, because my vices were Spanish, but my guilt was American. As the summer went on, I developed bronchitis.

There was never any reason to check the weather forecast that summer. The tanning beauties at the pool were like a farmer's almanac. Clouds are rare in July and August in Madrid, but whenever one appeared and blocked the rays the frustration was palpable. All present sat up, squinted at the sky, and glared at each other with the synchronicity of a musical number.

At the pool I heard such unadulterated gems of conversation that I cursed myself daily for not taking after the Spanish novelist Galdós and recording it to recycle later, to put them in the mouths of characters for the novel I wanted to write. I knew I had a story in me, and I often turned the tiniest fragments of life into stories when I talked to friends, but I was lazy and afraid of not knowing how to translate feelings into words on a page. I was not motivated enough. I was afraid of novelistic convention. I didn't like the concepts of plot, characters, or denouement. What worried me most was the ending. I could almost see myself *starting* to write but I could never imagine how anything would ever *end*, and this paralyzed me. Once when I was hired to give a series of lectures on literature, I realized as I prepared that I liked the beginnings of most novels the best. I often hated the way they finished, finding the endings contrived or flat. I was full of excuses for not writing. An Olympic procrastinator.

Mail from America arrived every few days, diverted from my empty apartment at the college, all of it official and some of it quite important. I stuffed it in a drawer, where it stayed for many weeks. I had a datebook. I used to love buying a new one every December and filling it with notes and plans with a fountain pen. For years I had organized my life meticulously: college, master's degree, PhD, always working at least two jobs. I had never wavered. I used to have nice handwriting and loved cheery, exotic ink colors. Lavender. Turquoise. My current calendar showed week after empty week. I didn't want to write anything down, though once in a while I grabbed some dry old Bic pen from the back of a drawer and made a note of a doctor's appointment in a jagged, sloping scribble. I was supposed to write an article on Franco and Hitler for a scholarly journal and had to ask for yet another extension. They were not appealing companions. The datebook gathered dust on my bedside table.

After the pool each day I went home to my room. I wasn't doing anything, really. Emails bounced in from my American friends. They reported on the weather, on their gardens. They said, "I hope the research on your book is going well. Have a productive summer." It was summer, after all. But I felt I had to keep up with my research and writing, I could never figure out if that summer was a vacation or not.

My mother's flat was full of paintings by her grandfather, and books, and other objects from the nineteenth century, some even older. The sheets in the linen closet were heavy linen and had my great grandparents' initials embroidered on them. How had these things survived? My mother usually rested in the afternoons. I tried to use that time to write articles and book reviews. In the evenings I went out with old friends or new random people or stayed in and cooked something for my mother.

I knew she was worried about me, and about how much time I was spending at the pool surrounded by women she called "the lizards." She pretended to go about her business, within her severe limitations, and gave me as much freedom as she could. She had always been resistant to the concept of psychology, and she was wary about the presence of Cohen in my life. I could almost hear her saying to herself, "This is just a phase, like when she turned four and wanted an orange birthday cake with purple frosting." Once in a while, when voicing an opinion about my life and my *psicólogo*—which sounded particularly lame to me in Spanish—she said, "What I think, and I imagine *your psychologist* would agree with me about, is . . ."

When I seemed worried, she sometimes shook her head in frustration and asked, "Do you really think this psychologist is doing you any good?" I didn't like the question, but I couldn't honestly defend the beneficial effects that therapy might be having on me.

I changed the subject. "In my spare time I am writing a novel."

She nodded. "That's a good idea."

I had a sip of wine. "I know, I just can't quite figure out what to write about."

She said, "Why not write about me? I've had a pretty interesting life."

"If I write about you, I would have to write about me. About our lives."

She shrugged. "Aren't many first novels autobiographical?"

13

MY OLD COLLEGE FRIEND ANNE invited me to visit her in Paris. Anne and I hadn't seen each other for a long time. We used to live together in the East Village and had a sister-like friendship. I suppose I was looking to rekindle that kind of bond with anyone who might have a clue about what I should do next.

She lived with her husband and young son in a sleek, rather impersonal apartment in the Fifth Arrondissement. Lots of stone and stainless steel—quite cold. They had a nanny. Both of them worked in fashion, but the husband had been an architect and he had designed the flat according to her specifications. The weather was gray, and I spent too much money on clothes in my favorite neighborhoods, the Marais, Abbesses, and ate Vietnamese food and steaks *au poivre*, or with béarnaise sauce, delights that were difficult to find in Madrid. I drank champagne. Anne was pregnant with her second baby and she was sleepy all the time. Once when we were sitting on the couch having drinks before dinner, she fell asleep.

Anne took me to adorable French baby clothing stores. She was a couple of years younger than me, but I felt she was light years ahead of me. After her rebellious late twenties, she had miraculously emerged as a graceful young mother and wife. It occurred to me that she was probably like this before college, where we had seemed so alike because we lived in dorm rooms and ate in the cafeteria together and liked the same boys. But we were not at all alike. She met her husband-to-be at a beautiful wedding in the French countryside, and together they bought this large apartment in Paris. She wasn't from Paris, yet she seemed completely at home there. Many of my friends have done this, in New York or Madrid, but few made it look so appealing and simple as Anne. I instinctively sensed

I would never find myself in her shoes, or anywhere near them. I watched her buy baby clothes, and she looked so lovely, considering and deciding between this or that little outfit. I knew that would never be me. Though I was still young, I reckoned I'd gotten the timing wrong, and that if I ever straightened my life out it would be too late. I would still be living in my New England village, not Paris, and I might be alone, and at the time it was very hard to see any silver lining in this, or how I might change my course. Convention, which looked so comfortable from the outside, had eluded me.

Everyone seemed very tough and thin in Paris, and the men and women had a more unique style than people in Madrid. I thought about the clothes I'd bought and how unhappy I would be if I got sick and had no money to look after myself properly because I'd spent it all on fashion. At least I would be beautifully dressed. Every time I went to Paris I wondered if I'd run into Philippe, a film director I briefly had a crush on years earlier, but I never did. I'd met him in New York and when he returned to Paris he sent me flowers, postcards, and two interminable handwritten letters, in broken English, about Lacan, and depression that I couldn't make heads or tails of. He said I was a "phantasm," or perhaps an angel, I can't remember. I agreed to see him when I passed through Paris a year later, but I was too shy to call him, and that was that. He lived near Pigalle, and despite the years that had passed I still associated the neighborhood with him and cheered up as I passed in front of the dingy cafes and sex clubs.

Paris was almost always as I liked it to be, in a way New York usually wasn't. I realized this had a lot to do with the fact that I had never lived in Paris, but only been there on vacations.

In New York I used to spend a lot of money and effort trying to match my experiences to the image I had, and often the image seemed just out of reach. This happened when I lived alone, and with other people. It was a time when it seemed a miracle could happen to us at any moment. But it never did. Miracles only happened to other people—a few degrees removed from my group. We had regular brushes with glamour and great success. I, in particular, was as good at attracting these opportunities as I was at repelling them. When I dated a boy from an interesting family, he was the disinherited black sheep; when a handsome film producer took me to dinner too quickly with his parents, I found it embarrassing and couldn't see him again.

But New York had advantages. Nobody cared where I was from. Nobody insisted that I was not really American, or not *really* Spanish because I was a mix. In New York I could be American, Spanish, Euro-something, or nothing at all. It was a great relief. In the time I had walked a block to buy a coffee from a deli, my path had crossed with a hundred people whose backgrounds were more complex than mine. Nobody asked that dreaded question that one of my students once put his finger on: Where are you *really* from?

14

BACK IN MADRID A WEEK later, Katya called and invited me to Marbella. I had to think hard about this. My mother thought it a tacky and potentially dangerous idea. My friend Mónica, who was a journalist and mother of two, thought I was crazy to hesitate. "Marbella at Mr. X's? A palatial house on the sea? Why wouldn't you go?!" She was always slightly disappointed in my lack of chutzpah. Okay. I was supposed to be having adventures and exploring life.

I took the train to Málaga and was picked up by a driver-bodyguard. I'd already met him in Madrid, where he and the others on the security team wore dark suits. At the train station I hardly recognized him in his Bermuda shorts and polo shirt, a small canvas tourist satchel hanging from his waist. I wondered if that was where he kept his gun.

Marbella's patent lack of values of any kind was the opposite of what my therapist and enlightened, progressive American friends held dear. Marbella was un-veneered capitalism and sunshine. It was the tomb of the romantic, and everything seemed, really, surprisingly simple. Desire, beauty, charm, lust, satisfaction—even fame—were all subservient to cash. Intelligence, originality, and style were superfluous. All that mattered for women was one's status as a luxury, duty-free object. The outfits, accessories, plastic surgery, and hair extensions could easily be computed, and all the men needed was the means to buy, or at least rent long-term. It was better to be a shop assistant at an expensive boutique, where you appeared luxurious and valuable by association, than to be a down-and-out aristocrat. Lineage didn't count—which may be democratic, I suppose—nor did education.

Their house was a contemporary-style villa on the water.

The butler showed me to my room and told me that the *señores*, Katya and husband, were playing tennis and would be back later. He pointed to the phone near my bed and told me to dial 26 if I needed anything. I tried to think of things I might need. I wasn't used to being in a guest room alone surrounded by armed men. I hung my clothes in the closet and tried to make myself at home. *Keep an open mind, Lola.* The floors in my room and bathroom were heated marble, and I walked back and forth many times to feel the warmth on my bare feet as I opened all the windows to let the garden air in. There were no books in my room. This was the kind of house people longed to be invited to, and yet I felt like I was in a creepy *Saturday Night Live* skit. Was there something wrong with me?

I went out to explore the rest of the house, wary of attack dogs and bodyguards, but there was no one, and no sound but the trickle from a fountain in the courtyard and some kind of Muzak that was piped through the vast rooms. I felt kind of like Nancy Drew, but there was no mystery to be solved. Off the courtyard on either side of an arched entrance were two identical mirrored bars, in a show of double excess—his and hers? The bottles and glasses were arranged next to silver bowls with mixed nuts and Fritos. It was too early for a drink, but I ate some Fritos, barbecue flavor, just because they were there. I took some from one bar and then from the other. I expected them to be limp and humid; in fact I *wanted* them to be stale. Perhaps they'd been there for a decade. But they weren't. These people knew how to keep their Fritos fresh and crispy, and someone was paid to make sure this was the case. I hadn't seen or eaten them since kindergarten. Who'd have thought that the wildly rich liked BBQ corn chips with their whisky? I did find some books, mainly unreadable: *Fifty Great Men. Keys to Success. The Beauty of Jewish Culture.* Then a variation on all of the above, wrapped into one great volume: *Fifty Great Successful Jewish Men.* However, there was one that looked good, and was: Philip Roth's *The Facts.*

The weekend was a parade of characters: the marquis that Katya was so excited about, who drank gin and tonics as if they were water; the owner of a nightclub; a real estate tycoon; the tennis pro with his girlfriend; and Katya's Pilates teacher. I understood, for the first time, what the expression "hangers-on" meant. I strained at conversation with the tycoon, and heard myself asking, with what was hopefully a cosmopolitan look in my eye, "How are you enjoying Marbella?"

I realized I would never make it in Marbella, and that I would never get to sleep. I left a lamp on, the furthest one from the bed, as I always do when I sleep alone, but that didn't help. It was a long night of intense anxiety, which I spent squinting at the Philip Roth book. I looked at the phone near my bed and wondered what the number for the local 911 was. Would they come if I called, or had they been bought off by Mr. X? Was I having fun yet?

By breakfast the next morning, my nerves were shattered. Even though it was early in New York, I needed a lifeline, and I called my old college friend Leah as soon as it was a decent hour in the States. She was an actress and had late nights, so it may not have been a decent hour for her. I was alone in the garden and happy to hear her voice. "Where are you?" she asked.

"I'm at Katya's house in Marbella."

"Marbella? Wow. Is it warm there?"

"Warm and sunny," I said. "Microclimate." I had just learned this fact and was eager to show it off. There she was at Whole Foods on Houston Street. I imagined the clear plastic containers of wholesome oat bran and raw cashews, the refrigerators full of soy yogurt, and I started to cry.

"Sweetie," Leah said, "I'm at Whole Foods, and you're in Marbella, and you're crying? What is wrong with this picture? Should I get on a plane and come join you?"

Somewhat comforted by her reliable humor, though mainly confused by the transatlantic connection to grocery shopping, I went back to my room. In the late afternoon I had a bath, and then dialed 26 to finally order a gin and tonic. A butler brought it and I started worrying about how much I would have to tip him when I left. I never knew about these things, and I didn't have much cash. Katya appeared and lay down on the chaise longue near my bed. I sat near the balcony in my robe emblazoned with the house's name—LAS PALMERAS—and smoked a cigarette. The marquis was coming for dinner and I had to do my hair and choose a dress, but after my sleepless night I didn't feel like doing anything. Katya picked one out for me, rushed off to change in her room, and soon we were having more cocktails and BBQ Fritos with the Marquis and Mr. X.

Mr. X liked the marquis, who knew how to amuse him. The Italian was a former pretty boy, with Alain Delon-like features, and was still good-looking in a ravaged way. We were stuck with each other for the night, but it didn't matter because we got along. It turned out, though we'd never met, that we were distantly related on my mother's side. He could play anything on the piano, and after dinner he played and I sang. Wow, I thought, I was literally singing for my supper. But I was a fool for music and for a few hours I forgot about the attack dogs, the possible guns, and New England. I had never sat down on a piano bench to sing to anyone, but I sat there that evening as if it were something I did regularly. We sang tunes that in any other context would have made me cringe, the most obvious Beatles hits like "Let it Be," Elton John and Kiki Dee songs. The marquis' musical evolution seemed to have peaked in the 1970s. We refilled our glasses with whisky, which I in fact hate.

In Spanish there is an expression, "*la mancha de la mora con una verde se quita*," literally "a ripe blackberry's stain can only be removed by a green berry." It's often just shortened to "*la mancha de la mora . . .*" and everyone knows what it means. The only way to get over past relationships is to meet someone new. I was in mourning over being alone, and apparently needed to try and move on. Thus the marquis, who might previously have seemed a comical character to me, was of interest simply by virtue of being a potential green berry. He was not for me, but through this fun evening I realized that someone would be again.

15

BACK IN MADRID, I STILL had to finish the research for my biography project. Not to mention the article about Hitler and Franco.

So I tried to get my work done, and to lie low like a chameleon in the jungle. At the same time, I still wondered about love. The candidates were not promising. Adventurous Leah in New York and Katya both insisted I try Facebook, but social media gave me the creeps, and I hoped to just stumble across someone in real life and fall in love. In a café. Someone reading an interesting book. Nobody thought this plan would work. The riskiest of the possible real-life people seemed to be the expat James, and—inevitably—he was the one who intrigued me. According to him, our perfect future was right around the corner. He made films and traveled. Six months in California, eight months in Paris or New York. Always just out of reach. He appeared and disappeared and had a style that I fell for repeatedly. Also, I had met him in real life. We had locked eyes across a room at a history conference. Or something like that. One of my oldest friends, Manolo, was fascinated that I had fallen for this man. He asked me lots of questions about him, and I lied in all my answers. At the time of this conversation James had disappeared and I was unhappy with him. "Is he handsome?" Manolo asked. "No," I said. This was not really true, but I was angry at myself and at James, and didn't want to even concede that he was very good looking. Was he tall? I shrugged. Tallish. He wasn't a basketball player or anything. Was he rich? No. Was he accomplished? No. Was he well educated? Nope. Was he kind? Most definitely not. I wasn't giving him any credit. Manolo rolled his eyes in awe and banged his fist on the table, saying, "This guy must be a *genius*! I wish I knew his secret." I love Spanish chivalry. My shrink said it was impractical to be interested in such a man, but Manolo praised James's talents.

James, originally from Dublin, had lived in Spain half of his life. He was bilingual and seemed to understand my Spanish and American sides. He had a sense of humor and a laid-back (too laid-back?) attitude. But I tried not to think about him and focus on what I knew: my work. I loved my research. Even though it would not solve any of my fundamental problems. The book that would result from it would put another feather in my academic cap and be published by a good press, bought by university libraries and reviewed in journals. As my sabbatical year sped by, I realized I had no choice but to return to Sheldon. The funny thing was that I missed Sheldon. I needed the academic calendar and my classes and my office just above the humanities library. That was me. I didn't see how I could have a dignified life and live in Spain; the two seemed mutually exclusive. Yet my mother needed me, and I liked having a family. My grandfather and Inés were gone, and only she and I were left. How could I leave her and continue to live on another continent?

I got to work and started writing Consuelo Marqués's biography. She had to leave Spain for the United States in 1939 and then spend her exile in Mexico. The more I learned about her life, the more interesting and complex she became. She had met Eleanor Roosevelt, Hemingway, and Malraux, and had married an aristocratic Communist pilot. Then she had died young in a car crash after World War II.

I kept some photos of Consuelo on my desk for inspiration. It had taken me over a year to track them down. One was of her with Stalin; another with Tina Modotti; and my favorite, one of her alone, smiling somewhere in Mexico dressed in traditional clothes, a la Frida Kahlo. My editor and one of my mentors told me that had she been prettier, the book would sell more. Men. Though she was not beautiful by conventional supermodel standards, I was always shocked when people brought this up. She was tall and had a radiant smile, great natural teeth, shiny brown hair, and large dark eyes. At one point I considered using Photoshop, but the truth was that I didn't give a damn about what she looked like. We had a deeper relationship.

I had a phone number for a nephew of hers who lived in Madrid, and I was hoping he'd let me interview his mother, Consuelo's sister, Concepción. I looked at the phone number for weeks. Diego Marqués. Every day I said to myself, *I will call.* Finally, one day I took a notebook to the pool and started writing questions for Concepción. I got excited. I was a bit nervous because the two sisters barely had any contact after the end of the Civil War, seventy years ago. Consuelo rebelled and fell in love with a Communist, and Concepción and her other sisters were pro-Franco.

I called Diego. He spoke very quickly, and I could hardly get a word in. I told him I would like to interview his mother. He asked me to meet him at a bar on the Calle Velázquez. I wanted to look professional, but it was over 100 degrees outside. I chose a new dress with pink flowers on it, below the knee, a bit retro fifties. I was really hoping this interview would go smoothly. The dress was lined in silk and the bodice was tight. It was truly too small, but it was so pretty and the only one, and it was on sale. As soon as I stepped onto the street, notebook in hand, I felt like I was wrapped in sausage casing. I wished I had money for a taxi and watched many of them zoom by as

I waited at the bus stop, thinking at least I'd have something useful for my progress report for the grant. *Interviewed subject's sister*. I loved the word "interview." I had never interviewed anybody before, and I suddenly thought of this as my new, blossoming Christiane Amanpour side. After the interview I would have a whisky somewhere glamorous. I didn't even like whisky.

Diego was in his late fifties, tall and handsome. From his clothes I could tell he spent more time in the country than in the city. The Marquéses had a huge estate in Extremadura. Bulls and horses. He was the human equivalent of a mud-splattered Range Rover. We had a glass of wine at the bar. I explained that I was a professor doing research on the Spanish Civil War. I mentioned, almost casually, that Consuelo had had an interesting role in the war.

He waved his hand and chuckled at my interest in his long-dead Communist aunt and paid, saying, "Let's go to my mother's house." The wine, the heat, my corset-like dress were all making me dizzy. We walked to Principe de Vergara, the streets ablaze with the white summer light of an August Madrid afternoon. The apartment building was regal, iron gates and a cool marble lobby filled with potted palm trees. The elevator had original wood and glass doors and a faded red velvet banquette and a mirror. When I was little, everyone seemed to live in these buildings, and I remembered going *de visita* with my mother, who would always have a comb handy for last-minute touch-ups in front of these elevator mirrors. Suddenly the elevator felt a bit tight. I was relieved when it stopped.

The flat was vast but dark, as if most of the rooms were never used. In the dimness I saw oil paintings, silk upholstery, and tapestries. I suddenly wished I wasn't there with this fast-talking boar hunter and my notebook. "Follow me," he ordered as we walked through the main rooms and a long hallway. Toward the end I saw light, and I followed him. He was yelling "¡Mamá! ¡Mamá! Look who I've brought to see you! *Una americana.* She's writing a biography of Consuelo!" I didn't know why he was yelling.

I finally saw her. Could this be Concepción? She was sitting in a beautiful straight-backed chair by the window. She was thin, with large eyes, high cheekbones, and long legs. She could have been painted by El Greco. Her thick gray hair was short yet abundant, and she was wearing trousers and a sweater. I felt terrible that she had no warning of our visit. Diego grabbed my arm and said, "I forgot to tell you, her health is quite good, but sometimes she's a little out of it."

I wondered if this was what Consuelo would have looked like had she lived to be ninety-eight. I wondered if this interview was such a great idea. Concepción started to speak. I thought she was asking who I was, but I really couldn't understand her. She asked me something I could not decipher. I smiled politely and said, "¿Cómo?" There was no air-conditioning. My notebook full of questions had become an absurd object. I finally understood what she was saying. "Do you have any news from Consuelo?" I was so excited to have understood this question that I nodded enthusiastically. "That's exactly right," I said. "I'm working on Consuelo."

"How is she?" she asked.

"She's dead . . . she died many years ago," I replied. She looked at her son, "Why is this person telling me that Consuelo is dead? Is it true?" My smile was straining. Before he could answer, I took Diego slightly aside. "She clearly wasn't expecting us. Perhaps I could see her another day, now that she at least knows who I am?" I followed him into another room. "Wait a minute," he said. He brought back two very old photo albums. "You'll find pictures of Consuelo here. You can use them for your book. Take your time. I'm going to take my mother out for some air." They just left me with the photo albums, alone in their home for a few hours. All the photos were from before the war, of course. I took photos with my phone, seeing the prim and proper upbringing Consuelo had, and wondered how she had strayed so far from her family, with two formidable parents and two sisters. When they came back, Concepción understood what I was doing, and she was very sweet to me.

When I got home my mother was sitting in the living room reading. She asked, with genuine curiosity, "How did it go?" I told her I would tell her later. "Weren't you hot in that dress?" No, I said, I was fine.

"Did they give you any useful information?"

"Great photographs. It was amazing to meet her sister. Her son was very nice."

I had a shower and lay down in my air-conditioned room. The air-conditioning was part of my American side, and my mother disapproved. Don't think Madrid is New York and you can just pop a Friedrich AC unit in the window and plug it in. It doesn't work that way. The windows are different, for starters. I paid 800 euros to have it installed, a process that involved three men and considerable drilling that I thought would bring the whole side of the building down.

Clearly Consuelo's sister would not give me much information, and this made my research all the more important. People who had lived through the periods I was interested in were elderly, if they were alive at all. I looked at my notebook. I looked at the copies of documents I had ordered from the historical archive of the Spanish Communist Party and the archive of the Spanish Civil War. I looked at all my notes from the books at the research center. Had Consuelo been murdered? Why did she become a Communist? What happened to her daughter? Did she ever see her family again once she left Spain? How did she adapt to her exile in Mexico? Why did her second husband leave her? Where were her papers? Who was going to answer these questions?

I passed a week rereading Consuelo's memoirs and tried to imagine her working in the foreign press office in Barcelona for the Spanish Republic. The Consuelo book took on a life of its own. I worked on it daily, piecing together bits of archival materials, conducting new interviews with people whose parents had known her, and gathering information from an ever-expanding collection of books that threatened to swallow up my bedroom. She had been so politically committed, had risked everything for what she believed in. She was a friend of Robert Capa, the dashing and brave war photo-journalist who had inspired the James Stewart character in Hitchcock's *Rear Window*. There were many gaps in her story, and trying to get to the bottom things became addictive.

I was trying to quit smoking and it wasn't easy while writing. I hated gum. It was probably not the best time to quit. Leah, my loyal friend who was holistic and vegan, emailed often from New York and offered more advice. She suggested cinnamon sticks for the smoking. I was intrigued, at first. I bought some, and the next time I wanted to smoke, I put a stick in my mouth. I tasted its cinnamon, woodsy flavor. I chewed. I thought about Inés. An email came in from Alex. "How's my favorite researcher?" There was a photo attached of him standing on the beach tan and shirtless, his hair longer and blonder, proudly holding a surfboard. I hit delete.

The cinnamon stick started to shred and filled my mouth with large, damp splinters. I attempted to push them to one side, but they seemed to be expanding and made me gag. I got up and spit them into the wastepaper basket, grabbed my bag, and counted my change as I walked, tears in my eyes, toward the cigarette machine at the grotty local pub. But it was Sunday and the pub was closed. I went back to the gum, plain old Spanish strawberry Chiclets, and started to write furiously. I never smoked again.

The great war correspondent (and Hemingway's second or third wife) Martha Gellhorn had been a close friend of Consuelo's. I was reading the Gellhorn diaries to see if she mentioned her, but she didn't. However, I discovered that Gellhorn—who I'd thought was tough and could laugh everything off—also suffered, and survived, and she became something of a role model for me. It was possible, apparently, to be eloquently lost, unhappy, and still live intensely.

16

VINOS CASA Gonzalez QUESOS
12 VINOS
QUESOS González FIAMBRES
12 VINOS
VINOS Y TAPAS

ONE NIGHT I WAS OUT at a small bar and cheese shop on the Calle León with Manolo and Mónica. The plan was to have a few glasses of wine and then hit a flamenco disco on the Calle Echegaray. I had met them both when I was a child. They were slightly older and each had kids, but every few weeks they would take a night off to hang out with me.

We were sitting at a small table in the corner, and suddenly I saw a young woman approaching me. It was dark and I couldn't see much, but she was definitely making a beeline for me and had a very pretty face and sweet smile. As she approached, she said "Lola?" I couldn't believe it. Nora, one of my closest friends from high school. We had stayed in touch through college, and had seen each other in New York and Boston a few times. But then we had been separated by life, boyfriends, geography. A few friends from school had come to Madrid with me during vacations, but Nora wasn't one of them. She was on a work trip and had just come into the shop to buy a bottle of wine. She ended up at the flamenco disco with us until three in the morning.

Nora had become an artist and lived in Brooklyn. Her trip to Madrid was supposed to be for a day or two, but her next big meeting in Paris got postponed and she was able to stay for a whole week. She came over to visit my mother, and I thought how ironic it was that we were all chatting away and having a drink together. So grown up. When Nora and I had last had a drink together, it had been behind our parents' backs hiding away in my room, or at a bar in Boston where we wouldn't get carded.

We spent several days together, and I took her to all my favorite places and even a flamenco class, which she may not have been as excited about as I was. We shopped in cool little stores in Chueca, and then went out to dinner wearing our new clothes. Just like high school. I showed her where we lived when I was little, and the beautiful street near the park where my grandfather grew up. As we walked around the city, we caught up on the snippets of information we had about people from school. We talked about our lives, the ups and downs. I told her all the things I had discovered about my family. Talking about it with someone who had known me for so long gave me perspective. She was also an only child, and her parents were still together. I remembered sleeping over at their house when I was a teenager. On Sunday we all went to mass early, by car, and then drove to breakfast at a coffeeshop. I had found this exotic.

Nora was close to her parents, but she had completely struck out on her own and eschewed the expected life choices. She had always been pretty, but instead of marrying the captain of the football team she had played bass in a band after college. Now she was an artist and made a living working in the art world. She had just bought her place in Brooklyn and was in a relationship with a painter.

Unlike many of our classmates, or people I had met since, she meandered and got where she was going obliquely. Her approach to life was a great relief to me.

Running into her that night reminded me of the power of kismet. It revived our friendship.

IT IS HARD TO MOVE to another country, even if it is your parents'—although I only knew one of those parents—even if it is where you spent time growing up. Because I have a Spanish name and was brought up speaking Spanish, my survival instinct drove me to try and fit in there, but very often I felt like a misfit who stood out like a sore thumb.

Being raised bilingual and studying and teaching language and literature had made me hyperaware of accents, rhythm, and intonation. Over the phone everyone assumed I was Spanish, but in person people always asked where I was from. "But were you *born* here?"

I was happy to lie in response to this obnoxious line of social questioning. It simplified things, and the question was simply too stupid to engage with honestly. I would not give them the satisfaction of letting them know I was born in the United States. I resisted at all costs their theory that this meant I was not *really* Spanish. Would I look more Spanish if I had been *born* in Madrid? I didn't look the way I did because of where I was born. Nationalism and logic had nothing to with one another. The other prize annoying question was what language I dreamed in. Some people feel really smart when they ask that one, and won't let it go until you've given them some definitive answer. The truth is, when you're bicultural (or tri, or beyond, as is more and more common) you can be very annoying to monocultural people. You can tell them you're either-or till you're blue in the face, but they will remain convinced you're neither-nor. It's all or nothing for many people.

Sometimes, I got a bit bored of Madrileños and their exclusionist attitudes, so eager to categorize everybody. I was frustrated that my perceived otherness was frustrating to them.

I still wanted to know more about my family's past. I had known since my teens that my mother raised me alone because she had to, and that my father had disappeared. They were together so briefly. Still, here I was, and I wanted more answers.

One day I went to visit Feli, our former cook, for lunch. She was in her eighties. The visit had been my idea. Part of me wanted to see her. Part of me didn't want to at all. The meeting took place at her modest apartment in Carabanchel. The minute I saw her in her black dress and apron as she opened the door, I burst into tears. I was reduced to being three years old again. I just looked at her, and tasted an overwhelming emotion. I couldn't believe I'd be expected to eat, but I had to because she was the cook and she had spent all morning preparing this meal for me. The feelings she sparked in me climbed up my throat and came out in endless tears. It was a strong force, and it came from her. It caught me by surprise. It was love, mixed with the irretrievable past, and secrets that could never be spoken. She had lived at my grandfather's house for forty years, so she had seen and heard everything. But she would never tell me anything. It was just her way. My mother and aunt growing up, my mother leaving and then returning with me and no husband. The past was so sad. I wouldn't press her. I respected her silence and dignity. But I wasn't quite ready to put it to rest yet. I had to dig a bit deeper, even if it had to be on my own.

The more I rummaged around in the boxes at my mother's, the more I discovered how tragic my family's story was, on both sides. The Spanish Civil War was responsible for nearly all of it. Everyone had been in the wrong place at the wrong time. Decades of weirdness followed. The Cold War era was a secretive one, and I had been raised on those secrets. Not that

I had any political significance, but the repression had deeply curtailed social freedom, and combined with the Catholic *franquismo* of Spain, my origins were slightly taboo. Or had been. Weren't things better now? Spain had been a democracy for over three decades. I had been educated to believe that I lived in a better time than my parents. If I at least tried to understand my past, would I be able to move forward?

Who was my father? I couldn't turn to my own memory. For me, he was an absence. I had been able to ask a few, very few, people some things about him, and now I was digging around in archives. I was aware that I had spent my life doing research about other people's lives, but for the longest time I had assiduously avoided looking into his.

One day at the archives I took a deep breath, and for the first time in my life I finally looked up his name in the historical archives I had access to. Once I got home, I stayed up late grilling my mother about him. I fell asleep looking for traces of him and his family on the internet.

I eventually learned that his father was originally from the Austro-Hungarian Empire, and that he had been an art dealer who started his career in Paris, but ended up in Madrid after the war of 1898 selling Spanish treasures to American millionaires. I liked the ring of that Austro-Hungarian Empire and decided to give this element a firm place in my identity. My father's mother was also originally from Eastern Europe, but her family had immigrated to United States. She was a stage actress, and they met in New York, and he brought her back to Spain, where he had a thriving business. I make a note that I had an American grandmother. He was close to many of the prominent Jewish families that had settled in Madrid after the Rothschilds began to invest in Spain in the late 19th century. Here things became a bit confusing. It seems that after my father was born in 1917, his mother ran off to England with a Shakespearean actor. She never came back. His father's young secretary moved in. They lived in the same neighborhood as my maternal, Spanish, Catholic grandparents. Just a few blocks away.

My father, from what I could tell, never saw his mother again. His father and step-mother had no more children. I don't know what he thought of the step-mother. My father was a talented pianist. When the Spanish Civil War broke out in 1936, he was already an established young musician, and living a bohemian life. He said he had been part of the theatrical troupe started by Federico García Lorca. I read that once when the actors were preparing to put on a play my father had been cast in a lead role. Lorca had wanted the role for himself, but decided he wasn't tall or slim enough. Then he realized, on closer inspection, that my father wasn't either. The part was given to a more slender fellow. This disappointment aside, my father had a precociously thriving musical career during the years of the Spanish Republic. Looking into his past hit home how much older he had been than my mother. My research was spanning nearly three centuries and suddenly I myself felt ancient.

My father was nineteen when Franco's military coup overthrew the Republican government, launching Spain into three years of bloody war. He was drafted to fight for the Republic, and was arrested and sentenced to death. His sentence was commuted, and he served a four-year term in various prisons.

Hitler was a close ally of Franco's, and the Nazis had a significant role in the devastation of the Spanish Republic. Picasso's *Guernica*, immortalizing the destruction of a peaceful

Basque village on market day by bombs dropped by the German Condor Legion, is perhaps the most famous reference to their alliance. During World War II, Franco's government was officially neutral, but the dictator was willing to do almost anything for his powerful German friend. Franco had complied with an order issued by Himmler that the Spanish government compile a list with names, professions, and addresses of Spaniards of Jewish origin. In May 1941, all the civil governors of Spain were asked to identify the Jews in their communities. The final list identified 6,000 people. Among them was my father's father. Though Franco did not, in the end, abandon his official neutrality. The 6,000 Spanish Jews were not deported to German camps, but they were contacted and had to register with the Spanish authorities, and the threat of being reported loomed large.

Because there were no official race laws in Spain, many Jews were officially charged as freemasons—part of the evil anti-Spain triumvirate along with Bolsheviks and Jews—detained, and sent to Spanish concentration camps. For my paternal grandfather, it was too much. If he was arrested he would lose his livelihood, already threatened by the war, and he feared deportation to a German camp. There were already several non-Jews in the wings eager to take over his share of the art market. He shot himself. His young secretary, who was Catholic and had already disappointed her family by going to live with a married man with a son, was unable to cope with the shame of suicide, and vanished. Someone had heard that she joined a convent in Avila and was never seen again. I went from having no paternal grandfather that I knew of to having one who killed himself because of the Nazi threat.

My mother had, tucked away, a photo of my father and André Malraux at an anti-Fascist rally in Valencia. Just the two of them, their left fists defiantly in the air. My father was so young. I also found an article about him from a Republican newspaper during the middle of the war, days before my mother was born. It praised his bravery and said that he had been wounded in the defense of a mountain pass. He was described as a valuable military officer and a conscientious anti-Fascist. I wished he had been a conscientious husband and father.

His prison term was served in several places. When he was finally released in 1943, he could no longer perform in Spain and his musical career was over. He was blacklisted, and for years he eked out a living. For a while he tutored wealthy children, like James Joyce in Trieste. The parents who hired him turned a blind eye to his political past. He also translated some books from English and German, his parents' languages. He made his way to the England where he could make a bit more money, and he eventually completed a PhD in Spanish Literature at Cambridge. I suspect that my father began to work for the Americans at some point, in the early 1960s. The CIA's Congress for Cultural Freedom had set up many initiatives in Europe, in Francoist Spain, and also in Latin America. But who really knows? From what I understand he was like a Zelig. One minute he was on Mexican television with Borges, another he was teaching at top American universities, next he was doing business in London and corresponding with Lord Bertrand Russell. I never found out where he was buried. I don't know why he ended up in Cuba. Everything that happened after my mother was of no interest to me.

How could I write a novel based on crumbs of information?

How to structure it? Could a family history be built on the disparate rubble surrounding two people, my parents, who had barely made it, like drifting debris, floating out of the apocalypse of 1930s Europe? Who wanted to know about them, or about their daughter, or the decades of difficult survival left in the wake of their ill-fated marriage? Who was I to write about a father I never knew? Did I really know any more or less about him than about my long-dead great-grandparents? But how could I write about anything else?

At the same time, the notion that I, Lola, had a personal connection to all this long-ago war, death, destruction, sin, and punishment made me see myself in a new way. I had always felt deracinated and fragile, but now I sensed I was hardy, like a tumbleweed hovering and blowing over the ground, bouncing year after year around the streets of a ghost town. I might just have time to write the story before the next big threat came along, which undoubtedly it would. I was in the business of recovering and preserving the past. My mother and I were both still alive. We had made it together across borders. As an immigrant to the United States, my mother had had to start from scratch and protect me, and she had succeeded against tough odds. We had kept so many secrets, and been quiet about so many things, that simply knowing more about the past and being able to acknowledge it was changing me.

I was eager to get back to New England and tackle the contents of the Samsonite suitcase I had in storage. For the first time I was immensely relieved I had all those letters. And after months of worrying about where to live back in Sheldon, I had found out online that the little red house was once again for sale. I'd made an appointment to see it the day after my return.

It was simple, small but pretty, on a brook, with a fireplace, within walking distance of my office, the tiny main street that was "downtown," and the museum that I walked to when I wanted to take my mind off things. There was a small barn on the property too. I didn't want to believe the house might be mine yet, but I had a good feeling about it. The idea of living there, teaching, and continuing to write in my spare time was appealing. One day I would make space for my Catalan grandparents' china.

18

IN JANUARY, I STARTED TO get ready to leave Spain for what seemed like the millionth time. I had put an enormous amount of energy into our small holiday preparations. I had done the shopping for food and presents, including an irresistible pair of pale gray silk pajamas with red piping I bought for myself. But the relief I'd hoped to feel after Christmas and New Year's was overtaken by a state of emptiness and sadness. The woman who took care of my mother had been gone for the holidays, and I had been in charge. Although that had made me anxious, the time alone had also brought my mother and me closer.

My eyes kept welling up with tears as I started to pack quietly in my room one morning before taking my mother her breakfast. We didn't speak of my departure. Why did I live so far away?

I put a cup of tea on her bedside table and warned her, in Spanish, "*Cuidado. Está caliente.*"

She smiled and said, in English, "Happiness is my daughter bringing me a cup of tea in her silk pajamas." She sighed, and once again told me, "You know, the day you were born it was snowing. I saw big fat flakes coming down through the hospital window, and it was only October."

**

A year later I was living in my very own red house. I was back to teaching. I was still writing my novel. And I was still seeing James off and on, long distance. I missed him.

One day as I was walking along the pretty trails in the woods near campus, I called my mother. We had transatlantic rambling conversations now, very much like the ones we had when we had walked everywhere together when I was little. I asked if she remembered the name of the couple she used to tell me about, the exiles who had lived in the shoebox-like house. Of course, she said, he was a very famous grammarian and librarian, Tomás Navarro Tomás. I realized it was the name of the library I used during my sabbatical in Madrid. I was also aware that nobody on earth at this particular moment but me probably cared to know who this man had been. I could already imagine an editor's pen crossing his name out in my manuscript with a query: "Relevance?"

I thought of all the institutions and streets named after someone of note we walk by every day without wondering or knowing who the person was. I thought of Tomás and his wife in their house in Northampton, Massachusetts, so close to where I now lived, and how I never connected him with the library in Madrid, even with all of those overdue book reminders.

That evening I looked him up on the internet. He was born in La Roda, Albacete, in 1884, and died in Northampton, Massachusetts, in 1979. Anyone could see that Albacete and Northampton don't go together. I remembered my mother saying how he wanted to be buried in Spain, but I assumed he was not. I wanted to find out.

It turned out Tomás Navarro Tomás was a major intellectual, a Republican, and that he ran the Biblioteca Nacional in Madrid during the Spanish Civil War. He managed to somehow protect all its treasures from the Francoist bombings. He was a renowned phonologist and had written dozens of classic studies about the pronunciation of the Spanish language. After the war, he was forced to go into exile. In Spain in the 1940s, he was purged, like my father, which meant he was unemployable, and his name was removed from his own publications. In exile he taught at Columbia University until his retirement. He and his wife must have moved to Northampton to be near their daughter, Joaquina, who chaired the Spanish department at Smith College. I looked her up as well, and was dismayed to see that she had died only a few months before, having lived to be 100. I could have spoken to her a few years ago. It was too late. It made me very sad. They seemed so much like us. Maybe we just had to believe we weren't exiles to survive. I found an obituary notice Joaquina wrote when her father died:

> *My father passed away on September 16, 1979, at 6:00 a.m. at Cooley Dickinson Hospital in Northampton, where we had taken him a few hours before, fearing that he was having a heart attack. It was actually a pulmonary problem, but it was just as fatal for the heart. Until then, he had stuck to his daily routine. He had even gone out to sit in the gallery every morning, from where he could see the garden. He loved the plants and the birds, and would talk about them enthusiastically. His magnificent memory was fully intact, as was his endless curiosity about everything. Every day he was grateful for the comfort and simplicity that New England offered, and for a life that was serene and pleasant.*[1]

Here I was. Still in New England. Still somehow the living legacy of those post-Spanish Civil War exiled generations that my parents belonged to. Would I also age in situ, peacefully admiring my garden until I died?

---

1 *Evocación de Don Tomás Navarro Tomás*, Luis Flórez. *Thesaurus*. Tomo XXXV. Num. 1 (1980). Centro Virtual Cervantes.

A few days later, on August 17, I received an unexpected email from my mother. Though I often wrote to her, it was hard for her to type, and I had an unsettling feeling when I saw a message from her in my inbox:

Subject: Barcelona
Atentado terrorista en las Ramblas al lado de la Boquería, furgoneta arollando a gente. Siguen informando. Besos.
(Terrorist attack on the Ramblas by the Boquería market, a van is running people over. Developing story. Kisses.)

I called her immediately. I could hear the TV news booming in the background.

After we spoke I thought of las Ramblas, imagining it packed to overflowing with tourists taking pictures on their phones, drinking wine and beer. I thought of the locals running their stands at the Boquería market, a celebration of fruit and vegetables, all the varieties of fish, cheeses, and charcuterie. The market was near the Liceu opera house, just blocks from my maternal great-grandparents' former home. My great-grandparents who had been swept into the Spanish Civil War with three children, and had come out with none. Their only consolation had been their two granddaughters, my mother and Inés.

My mother spent many periods of her life in Barcelona with her grandparents until they had both died when she was in her early twenties. She frequently used their box at the opera, dressing up in an old black astrakhan coat of her mother's. Her grandparents (and their relatives) were all Catalán, and they spoiled her, their young and motherless granddaughter.

She was eighty years old now, and as she watched the nonstop news on the Spanish television about the attacks in Barcelona, she saw how the van entered las Ramblas and drove down toward the market. She saw the streets of her youth.

I couldn't bear to watch any videos of the attack. I looked at some photos online. One image stuck with me: an elderly couple that had been mowed down, still clutching their plastic supermarket bags from Carrefour Express.

19

I REMEMBER MY MOTHER PREPARING her classes on *Guernica* and the Spanish Civil War at Middleton College, between the burlap walls of our apartment over the garage.

My room in Madrid was still full of the boxes with all the pristine china from Barcelona, including the pieces used only once, for my grandparents' wedding.

I'm walking around my backyard in New England. I'm on the phone with my mother again. I'm looking at the hydrangeas I planted when I bought the house. I love them, and they have somehow helped to make Sheldon my home. Their trunks are still slender and pliable, like a newborn pony's legs, and last night's rain has knocked them down. I keep meaning to get posts to hold them up. It's peaceful here in this garden, but it is quiet and isolated. When I have free time, I take walks around the pretty parts of the town and admire the grand old houses and the lawns. At the same time, I miss seeing people on the street. I miss Spain.

History is so weird. The flowers in my garden remind me of a building on a leafy central avenue in Madrid. Today it is a nursing home and the elderly sit outside in the courtyard, which has a garden full of robust hydrangeas and rosebushes. The building was a prison during the war. My father was there for a year or so, and at least one of his close friends died there. It was later turned into a convent, and is now a home for the elderly. Variations on a theme. There is a small plaque on one of the walls, but its place in memory is tenuous at best.

James visits me, and I'm thinking about how to tempt him to stay for a while. After many years in Spain, he is actually looking forward to coming back to America to be with me. We take a walk up a picturesque hill. It's always a bit hotter and more humid in New England than I would like. He loves my house, and thinks Sheldon is quaint. But he worries about my small-town life. I tell him I'm never bored here because I teach all day and love my classes and in the evening I work on my writing. I have some friends. I have a fireplace. He is not convinced. "Shouldn't you do other things in the evenings? Go out? I think of you as a bit more urban."

We've reached the top of the hill at this point. The views are very beautiful. I look up at James and ruffle his hair and say, "This is my land. I'm both. Or neither."

We kiss. Nobody can see, I hope. Down below there are dozens of church steeples in Sheldon and the next town over. I look at him and ask, "Are you thinking what I'm thinking?"

He nods. "I've never seen so many churches in my life, and I've been around the block. I think we need to get you out of here." I tell him I like seeing all the steeples. I look up for another kiss, which is cut short as I see someone I know marathon-training and pounding up the hill, her face red with exertion. I pull away from James, but the kiss has had its effect. I feel dizzy and happy. James asks, "What's that smile about?"

I ask him, "Have you ever heard of the kissing disease?"

He frowns. "Isn't that what they used to call mono?"

"Yes," I say, "but to me it means something else. Anyway, I think I have it. Maybe."

James leaves, and once alone in Sheldon, I vow that on my next trip to Spain I will properly pack up the porcelain tigers and nymphs and ship them to New England. They will be displayed in my small house, with all the china and glasses, somehow, somewhere. Even as I think about this, I sense that these objects will only be in America temporarily, before we all, finally, go home to Spain together.

It's late August and my mother is virtually alone, across the ocean in her Madrid building with her caretaker. She meets two friends at a shady bench in the late morning before lunch.

She tells me, by phone, that both her friends, who have children and grandchildren, are selling off their china, linen tablecloths, and silver. "Their kids don't want these things. Nobody will ever use them again. And they're not even worth much. They were our treasures."

James calls me a few days later. He says there has been a change of plans, which makes me anxious. It turns out he will be shooting a film in Barcelona the following year. He asks me to move there with him. He's always wanted to live there—but, he says, only if it can be with me. I can't take another sabbatical so soon, so I would have to leave my job or ask for an unusual leave of absence. I don't think I can do this, but a glimmer of irrational light appears in my imagination as I realize that I might very well want to move to Barcelona and see what happens. James reminds me that the AVE fast train can take me to Madrid in just over two hours, so I can see my mother whenever I want. No driving involved. He asks if I'm afraid because of the recent terrorist attacks. No, I'm not. In fact, if anything, they have made me feel closer somehow to Barcelona. His movie is about the tensions around Cataluña's Independence movement, and I know things won't be easy there in the near future. And yet, I want to go. With him. What if this is what I have always wanted, without knowing it?

We decide to talk the next time he comes to visit. As it turns out, the financing for the film gets delayed, and he comes to

Sheldon to live for several months. He starts working on a novel set in Ireland. He has to travel back to Spain every once in a while, but, much to my surprise, he loves New England. He ships over most of his things, which are very few. He is a bit of a Spartan, unlike me who never has enough closet space for clothes and shoes. For my birthday he gives me a black-and-white Tibetan terrier that we name Paco. Every day that they can, James and Paco walk up the long hill from where all the steeples are visible. James finishes a book about Spain he had been working on for a few years, and the Spanish consulate in New York organizes a reception for him. We buy a car and drive around the countryside. We go to Middleton one weekend, and I show him the house with the apartment over the garage. We have dinner with Edith, who is retired and lives nearby on a farm. In Sheldon, James and Paco are more sociable than I am, and we have started to see more of a few people that I already knew and others I had liked from afar. We become a small family. Everything, including going to the supermarket in a car, becomes fun.

Just as I start to worry that we are getting too comfortable in Sheldon and will never get back to Spain, James's producer says that the money has comes through. The plan is to start shooting in Barcelona a few months later. By now it is clear that we will not move there, but I manage to take a semester off to go with him. When the time comes, we fly to Madrid first, with poor little Paco in cargo, and visit my mother as we look online for short-term pet-friendly apartments in Barcelona.

I start dreaming about a large apartment with high ceilings where all the porcelain will finally have a home—where it actually came from. I know this doesn't make sense because it is temporary, but I can't help dreaming about Barcelona. I go to the Catalán bookstore on the Calle Alcalá in Madrid and buy materials for a crash course in the language. I start to drive James crazy with the repetitive audio.

"You know, you don't have to learn Catalán, you'll just pick it up," he says. He just picked up Spanish, but I am different.

"I'm sorry to be so uncool," I reply, "but this is actually really fun, and when we're there I'll have entire conversations and you won't be able to understand a word."

On one of our last days in Madrid I go to the Biblioteca Nacional to print out a couple of articles I need for my research. My old ID has expired, and I am dreading the complications of getting a new one. As I start to explain who I am and what I need to the guard at the front desk of this vast, majestic library, she gives me a sheet with descriptions of the different cards I can apply for. As I scan the paper, searching for the one with the least red tape, I see "Author." I tell the guard, "I am an author." She asks if my book will come up in the library holdings. I nod. She plugs in my name, sees my book, and I instantly get my fanciest card ever. The last time I used this library I had never published anything.

I leave all my things in the required locker. The digital databases have been modernized since I last used them, and when I sit down at the computer in the beautiful reading room, I download the articles I need. Just before logging off, I type in my father's name. I have done this before and am prepared to find nothing. However, the search pulls up something new: four studio photographs of my father, aged eighteen or nineteen. He looks so luminous, young, and handsome. The photos look like headshots of a 1930s screen idol. I click on the order box and request the highest quality reproductions. My father before the war, before his family was destroyed, long before meeting my mother, before America, before disappearing. I won't frame the photos, but I keep them close to me.

As I leave the marble halls and walk toward my locker to pick up my bag and coat, I see a newish plaque on the wall. It is quite large, and as the letters come into focus, I recognize a familiar name: "On the occasion of the exhibit 'Library at War,' the Biblioteca Nacional pays homage to its director during the years of 1936–1939, Don Tomás Navarro Tomás, and to all the librarians who, in such difficult circumstances, were able to preserve this legacy."

Before I go home to have dinner with James and my mother, I walk out of the library and head toward Cíbeles and onto the Gran Vía. The streets are crowded and thronged with tourists, people on e-scooters, and Madrileños going about their business. It is sunny and I can't help smiling as I think that I have unexpectedly found new bits of my father, and that Tomás Navarro Tomás, who died in far-off New England, has finally been honored at his library. I call James and he asks how the *biblioteca* was. "Amazing," I say. I realize I am walking by Chicote, the bar where Hemingway, Martha Gellhorn, Langston Hughes, and other foreign correspondents hung out during the Spanish Civil War.

James sounds puzzled. "The library was *amazing*? Did you get what you needed?"

"Yes, and so much more. I'll tell you later. And no, I haven't lost it. I think I'm done with my personal research for now. I'm just taking a walk on Gran Vía and I love it. In fact, do you want to meet me at Chicote."

"I'll be there in ten minutes. Actually I have to pick something up nearby, so that's perfect."

I know that I won't be back to the archives again anytime soon, not to look up my own family, at least.

The past that destroyed so many people will always overshadow my life. The 2020s or 2030s will never be free of the 1930s, or the 1960s. I know the china might break in shipping, that we may be lost in whatever history brings next, that someone will get my obituary wrong, or that I may never have one. I may never know where to be buried. Nobody might remember my mother or me, or my family's complicated histories; our lives in two countries where we never knew what would come next, and nothing was ever as it was supposed to be.

James arrives at Chicote and we kiss. We sit at a table and he goes to the bar to order martinis. I people watch through the window, and also look at him as he walks back toward me. The waiter brings the drinks. James says, "I know you prefer olives, but this one has a . . . twist." I look down at my drink, see a glimmer, and fish out a ring, white gold with a crescent of diamonds. It looks like an antique design.

He clears his throat. "It was my mother's. And yes, I want to marry you. But you don't have to answer now."

"What? Was that a statement or a question? Anyway, I don't have to wait to answer. Yes!"

I dry off the ring and put it on my finger. It has just been cleaned and polished at Grassy, the old jeweler right on the Gran Vía. He has picked it up on the way to the bar.

James smiles. "We can do something very low-key."

I look alarmed. "Why?"

"I just thought you might prefer that. Eloping or something. I'm happy either way."

I shake my head. "I might have preferred that in the past. No more subterfuge for me. I want a proper wedding. Don't ask me what that means right now. It can be simple, but everyone who counts has to be there. And it has to be in Madrid... Or in Massachusetts. Or..." How could I ever choose?

Barcelona, January, 2020